# The Voices Are Real

D.K. Dillenback

# The Voices Are Real

For Lee.

# CONTENTS

# IT ISN'T REAL

Cheryl. My Cherry, I let Cherry leave. I let the kids leave. Nothingness turns to fog, which turns to haze, and I'm suddenly aware of my existence. Warm and floating and painless in an unknown void. There is no shape, no time, no thought. Just existence: simple, infinite, and meaningless.

I am not myself; hell, I'm not even I. But I keep saying I. So, "I" exists. I keep saying words, so words and language exist. I'm speaking in English, so English exists. But before I have words to express it, the pain emerges from nothing. The slow, dull reintroduction of misery begins. My toes hurt, so I must have toes. I'm gradually becoming aware of my body. Pain sketches it out and brings it into focus. The universe does not hurt, so I am not the universe. This slow drum of torment carves me from the infinite void and shapes me into a small, bipedal ape.

I'm human. I've been human before. I am not the universe. Who am I?

I chuckle at a fake riddle. So, actual riddles must exist. As should real people and jokes and relationships and laughter. One by one, I remember what existence is, and each item, in turn, begins to exist. I see the shapes of people and animals and cars and trees form in front of me. They swirl in the shapeless void and bear no relation to each other. But that's not how reality works, right? My eyes must be closed (oh right, I forgot about eyes), and I am imagining the shapes.

But the pain is real, so my body is not in my mind. Well, I suppose pain is entirely in the mind though. So, pain itself is no indicator that my body exists. Have to run some tests. I think of the pain. It has spread and diversified, carving me out of infinity into a fleshy sack of bones and organs. My head throbs, but I feel pressure at my back. In fact, I feel pressure all along the back of my body. The pressure begins to orient me in the void, and I discover gravity.

Suddenly, I'm lying down. Well, I suppose I was lying down the whole time, but now I can feel it and understand it. I am not in an infinite void, but this feels more like an overdose of oxy. I feel gravity, though it's a little stronger than usual. I suddenly feel my fingers and strain to move them.

A light tap on my thigh. I should try again to make sure that was me. I wiggle again three times.

*Tap, tap, tap.*

So, I've found myself. I am a human, lying on the floor after taking too much oxy, maybe morphine or heroin, I suppose. What the hell is my name? I should have a name, right? It'll have to wait right now. Best not to strain too much.

The haze is lifting, and I begin to feel temperatures. My legs are warm and numb, but my torso is cold. As I shift my body little by little, I begin to feel the friction of sand or dirt scraping my skin beneath my body. A dirt floor? Or at least a dirty floor. Certainly not the beach. Cold and rough and filthy, like the decaying concrete slab of Dad's garage the night we left. He huddled over a small, nondescript piece of whatever poor motorized appliance or motorcycle or car couldn't escape his prying hands. That one feeble light bulb is hanging from a rafter on a length of rusted picture wire, crudely bent into a hook, creating deep tunnels of contrasting light and shadows. There he is now! Leaning awkwardly to the side to get light into the deepest crevasses of the lawnmower motor. I'm seven, watching from the icy driveway in the dark Vermont night. Mom shoves me quietly into the car, and as she covers me with a blanket in the back seat, the dome light of the old Subaru illuminates her bruised face; the small cut on her lip is no longer bleeding, but the glistening lines of tears show just how swollen her eye had become.

I see dad in the mirror. He glances up only briefly at the car but says nothing. He turns his head back downward and searches for some tool to pry or twist, or likely break, the metal patient on his operating table. I smell the burning exhaust of the car as mom accelerates out of the driveway for the last time. I can smell it now. But it twists into something new, and I am back in the present. Carving myself out of this eternity.

My smell returns to the present with a sour and complex mixture of sewage, roadkill, and honey. The kind of toxic bubblegum sweetness of New York City, walking by roasted nuts and a subway exit. Wherever I am, it is not a warm bed in a safe home with a loving family.

I hear the distant drone of a fan. No, too loud; it echoes through far-off chambers. Its uniformity is a lie. Rushing water? A faint clang! Clang! Clang! Something metal, something hard. Something violent. And suddenly, I feel fear. A lingering sense of impending doom. Luckily, it's far away for now. Within my small space, the deafening silence of a corridor as the echoes of every little breath scatter across the walls, filling the room with white noise. My ears are ringing loudly, but I can hear.

I'm suddenly aware of my breath, slow and steady, but being as fickle as breathing can be, it becomes faster and more painful as I become aware of it. Broken ribs maybe? Sharp pain at the peak of each inhale.

Slow down… stay calm.

As putrid air fills my lungs and my body yearns for more, my mouth opens, and I can taste. A faint, metallic taste of old blood maybe? My mouth seems misshapen. A lump has formed in the right cheek. Is it swollen? I tongue it.

"Fuck, that hurt." It's definitely swollen. I press harder and feel a pop. "Fuck, abscess" The infection bursts into my mouth. Filling it with the rotten, diseased puss from, I assume, a now-burst sore. The taste of death, and I begin to choke.

I'm wrenched back into existence. Heaving my body to the side, I roll all my weight onto my shoulder and wretch, vomiting on the floor in front of me. My body seizes and heaves, and I feel it coming. Tunneling from my gut to my mouth with each spasm. God, I miss that infinite void. As vomit sprays out in front of me and clogs my nose, I notice the terrible pain in my now flattened arm. It's broken.

I can open my eyes and witness the carnage of my wretched existence. It's dark. The faint gray of dawn fills a small, dust-caked concrete chamber, but I can't locate the source.

There is more rattling and clanging in the distance. It's closer now.

Squinting so hard my eyes start to shake, but I can't see. The grey light cannot distinguish other forms from the void. But it glows enough to show me it's there. Useless. It binds me to this reality and reminds me that I'm in pain. But only the pain itself etches out the forms around me. I look at a hand; that hand does not hurt me; that hand is not mine. I look down at a lumpy, heaving ribcage. It cauterizes my synapses with every halted and slow inhale. That torso is mine. I am breathing.

The grey stays the same, but my eyes begin to hurt and, thus, reaccustom themselves to the darkness. The empty shadows lurk on the edge, but colors glow faintly against the abyssal darkness. Maybe the room isn't that small. I roll off my injured arm and stair at the ceiling, swallowing the last chunks of dark vomit that clear my nostrils and fall to the back of my throat. I'm calm enough to feel the relief. The immense pressure gone from my face. Small blessings, I guess. God, I miss the void. Close my eyes and try to sleep. The weight of my chest suffocates me, and I try to die. If that was death, so be it.

But the void stays beyond my grasp and fades ever further away. I am stuck here, in this putrid and rotten body, aching in pain and prostrate, ready for oblivion.

But, like the void, oblivion doesn't come; it hovers and threatens and teases closure. It makes my suffering sharp and salient. So, sooner or later, I'll have to do something. What's that? The noises have drawn closer. The heavy, clanging thud of metal and the scrape of something pick on gravel and concrete. Wet, popping creaks of something from deep below the surface, under the water and filth that coats the skin of this horrible world. God, I miss the void! I'll have to just wait for death.

But Cheryl. OH, Cheryl! My eyes close, and I feel the expansion of fire in my heart. Pouring over the edges and bursting through my arteries. The grey is not so dim; I close my eyes and think of Cherry, desperately trying to hold onto my one happy thought. I close my eyes, and her dazzling image appears before me. Suddenly, I am clear. I know who I am. Reggie is my name. Her name is Cheryl, and she's the most beautiful girl in school. I loved her since the moment I laid eyes on her at Sadie Hawkins. I went with my older sister's friend whatshername. I didn't want to go, but I think she felt bad for me at the time. I was new and quiet and awkward, and Sadie Hawkins was less about getting a date and more about helping the new and quiet and awkward kids get out of their shells. God, it was uncomfortable; I came out of oppressive politeness (I had never told a girl no before), and she invited me out of aggressive politeness. But that didn't matter when I saw Cherry as I perched up on the bleachers and stared across the gymnasium. She wore the same shimmery dress that she wore on our first date two years later. She laughed with friends and grabbed a handful of cheesy crackers off the snack table.

I sat and watched and waited, and we became friends over the years. I somehow convinced her I was worth taking out on a date. Sometime later, I convinced her to marry me. And then there were drinks and celebrations. There were kids and drinks and more celebrations and arguments and love and drinks. Then darkness. More drinks, more parties, less kids, less family, less Cherry. More arguments, more drugs. God, it was all with me again. I exist, and I am worthless. My chest heaves and gets heavier. I try to die, to will myself to die. To tell my heart to stop. But it slows and calms me and keeps beating. God, I miss the void!

I let Cherry leave. I let the kids leave. I hated myself, and I watched that hated-me shoot himself up with anything within arm's reach. God, I should be dead. What God would bring me back?

The dragging, scraping, and clanging draw near. Please be death.

I drank until I had nothing left. My sister took Cherry in, and they abandoned me to the streets. It was more than I deserved. At least the kids are safe; I hope they have a better shot with a dead dad than with me. I am a testament to the failings of humanity.

But Cherry, she said something the last day. God, what did she say? She said, "I hope that someday you're human again."

I just want to die.

But I can't die.

No.

I have to live; I have to see them again. I have to be human. I am human.

I open my eyes. I see the concrete ceiling cracking and breaking apart to reveal the brick underneath. I smell sewage and roadkill. The roadkill could be any meat that has fallen into this hole with me. Hell, it could even be me if I'm septic. But sewage is sewage. There is no way around it. I'm in a sewer or storm drain. Or at least near one. I'm underground. There is no light, but somehow, I can see the ceiling. I crane my neck and look around to my left. The bricks disappear quickly into a tunnel, dark and abyssal. To the right, a faint glow ricochets through the halls, illuminating the grey walls. A dream or moonlight? Salvation or mirage?

I can feel my body now. It is rotten and swollen and a burden. But it's what I have. I slide my good arm along the floor and find a place to push myself up into a hunched, lurching silhouette. The angle is too much, and I vomit again. The balance is too much. I am dying.

The wet, scraping, and banging noises have slowed, but I hear the echoes resounding through rock and bone, keeping the threat of danger ever present in the room. The air begins to hum and shake. There is something here... with me.

How long have you been watching?

No. It's nothing. I have fallen and need to get moving... of course, I'm hallucinating. I'm a fucking junky. What is that shape? It's just beyond darkness, just out of reach. It stares with fish-bowl eyes just beyond the darkness. Glinting, watching me. Does it breathe? Is it alive? I am still.

Don't breathe…

Just… don't.. breathe…

My head is clear. For the first time, I hear silence pounding at the gates. A silence that holds desperately against the fear. But there is nothing here. I try to stop the harsh shivers in my chest as I force in just enough oxygen to survive. I want to move, but I can't. I wanted so badly to die, and now I am petrified.

There is… nothing… there. You're fine. But then why can't I – *what was that?* A faint chime? The micro-scratching of a scared insect. Like a lone cricket desperately searching for the comfort of a mate. The terror, it's there. I feel its breath and smell its hunger. It shifts and scuttles from the darkness. But the darkness follows it like the clouds of death. So fast, but it's silent? Is it drowned out by the rushing clamor that begins to echo through the chamber? Legs glint in the light, smeared with mud and filth like defensive wounds from a drowning victim. From the pointed feet, no, not feet. Claws? A scuttling demon from the deepest parts of the world. Its fangs and mandibles squittering in excitement as it scurries through the dark toward me. Maybe if I play dead?

I try not to breathe. I feel the warm tears stream down my face as I try to lower my torso as quietly as possible. The rib is surely broken. The terror moves and shifts and squeezes itself along the tunnel. The wet chirping echoes through the halls like hungry bats in the night. And it approaches. I'm lying still now. Praying and thinking of Cherry in her beautiful and shimmering dress. How did I let myself ruin her life? How many thousands of chances did I have to make things right? How could I ever see her again?

I feel my body now. When did my skin return? A cold, hard arm caresses my abdomen, pausing at my armpit and sliding along the length of my arm. That horrible chirp, I feel it in my bones. Don't wince…

Don't… fucking… move! Animals don't eat dead things, right? It works for bears or something, right? I feel the swift and refined grip of the long claw on my wrist. God, just play dead. Animals don't eat dead things. Please, god, let this thing leave me be. Let it think I'm rotten. I am rotten after all. I'm rotten and decaying in my shell. That's it, this isn't real. This is hell, and I'm already lost.

The demon claw held so lightly, the pressure built along the wrist, admiring God's handiwork. Caressing gently as if not to damage my filthy arm. It paused…

This is hell; I've already lost. I'm suffering for the wrongs I've perpetrated in life. At least I know now. There is a just God. A just God would want me to suffer.

Still, it paused… for minutes or hours. I try not to breathe; I beg my heart to stop beating. This isn't real. So why am I still afraid? I have nothing left to give. I open one eye, hoping to see the dejected monster turning away to something more alive.

Eyes. Eyes staring back at me. It sees me, and it sees my soul. It knows I'm alive, and it strikes. It feels like a baseball bat. My body begins to jerk, and I feel it now, the fiery burn of the flesh, shorn from the bone. But my body jerked; it couldn't get through. I'm screaming now. It raises again, faster this time. The gut-wrenching crack, and my arm is numb. No, not numb; there it is above me. The thing reels backward with the sudden release of tension and chirps as it takes my arm in its mandibles, licking the blood as it sprays over its terrible head. I'm screaming and heaving, but wait. This is hell, and I'm already lost. This is hell. It isn't real.

# PSYCHOSOMATISM

Fear doesn't come from the unknown. Fear of the unknown comes from fear of powerlessness. This is the same fear posited by Thucydides' description of the Peloponnesian war. It's a fear that drives mid-life crises, motivates preemptive war, triggers Post Traumatic Stress Disorder, and provides the motivation for religions seeking to offer a comforting explanation to the creeping dread of existence.

*-- From the Notes of Stacey Travers attending a lecture given by Dr. Harriet M. Sackler (Ph.D.), "Origins of Motivation," presented at Boston University on April 12, 2017.*

Down. Go down, son.

That ringing. That same desperate ringing in my ears. More than the faint whisper of tinnitus left over from years ago. No. This ringing, shrieking that rattles teeth and sends shockwaves down my spine like a dental drill. That noise passes through the air and body like radiation poisoning the soul. It is like the braying and screeching of a thousand tortured animals. It shakes and condemns and comforts and cuts. It engulfs his being and merges all senses into one death knell, signaling oblivion at the gates. Every time, it was a little more potent. It lasted a little longer, like something was coming.

That's what Cyd told himself when he was alone in the quiet tomb of his home. But never to anyone else. Who would listen? The world is supportive right up until you claim to know the future; then you're crazy. He had been suffering for years now without relief. But psychosis festers. It creeps up when least suspected. When the host is least on-guard. Now, it's accelerating. Every seventeen days, it hits like a clock.

My head wants to burst. My brain pushes against the lining of my skull, slowly crushing itself into paste against its own protective shield.

*Go down. Deeper. I need help. I need you.*

The same voice, rasping against the air as if oxygen burns its lungs. It's always pleading… except when it's commanding.

*Go down, then deeper until you find me. Down and deep, always deeper, son.*

"Wake up." No, it never tells me to wake up. I can't wake up. I'm not asleep. "Yes, it's me, you need to wake up. Are you still with me?" Every. Single day, I live the nightmare of the next coming cycle.

*I stared into her eyes and soul every day. I withered away, feeding her and staring into the darkness. It never receded, not once.*

"CYD!"

Cydnie was startled and was suddenly aware of his existence. Was he lying down? No, sitting. Where? Feeling the hard wooden chair with one short leg and listening to the busting sounds of the room come into focus. Sharp clinks of metal on ceramic coffee cups. The strained whisper of a father disciplining his arguing kids. But where did his name come from? And the bricks of that scratching voice assembled themselves into someone familiar. Where was he?

Diner. Coffee. Why is it always a god damn diner? Doesn't anyone meet in bars anymore? He opened his eyes at the black abyss beneath his nose. No, not abyss, just coffee. His head rested in his hands. Eyes up. There was James. He had asked to meet up. James was the one asking these days, but the invites were less frequent. He had gained weight, a 'sympathy belly' earned over the course of many late-night trips to the grocery store for pickles, or peanut butter, or ice cream. James' eyes were soft and tired. He met with Cyd out of a sense of love and responsibility, but there was a wall between them. Cyd noticed the silky, warm air waft from his cup to his nose, and he felt his pulsating migraine subside ever so slightly. It must have been some time since his last dose of caffeine.

"So, they're getting worse?" James asked. "How long has it been this bad?"

"Hard to say. What day is it?"

"The thirteenth."

"Is it still September?"

"No, October thirteenth."

"Damn." Cyd felt a weak smile tighten his face. "So, like, three months now."

Cyd loved and hated his brother James since college. They weren't related, but they were brothers like the old social cliches of childhood. Friends plus time multiplied by drama equals the chosen family. Cyd was comforted by the concept at first, having no significant blood relatives anymore, but over time, this became less of a chosen bond and felt more like a desperate grip on humanity. They spent years drinking to oblivion, wandering dark streets at night, cursing everything and everyone they could think of. They were terrible for each other, always able to push themselves a little harder, drink a little more, and find the seedier acquaintance with the better drugs. But it got stale. When they were young, nothing mattered because they all thought they were going to die anyway. When they didn't, they had to learn to move forward. Slowly, time ground onward. Relentless and cruel. The world didn't care about their dreams. James got a job and started setting goals. The first time he refused to go out felt like a divorce, leaving Cyd to drink alone and wander until he woke up missing a shoe in the bushes outside his apartment. James met Sarah, and they began to grow. Cyd and James grew, but not together. Cyd met Becca smoking a clove cigarette outside some basement club. She was new and dangerous and talked about colors and sounds in a way that made them feel fresh and alive.

James began to pretend he was getting better. A show for Sarah and the life she represented. Calm, content, and stable. Cyd followed Becca from basement to hovel, to abandoned factory, to river shallows wrapped in a miasma of lust and drugs and whiskey.

Now, they were separate. Years had passed, and adventures spouted and veered and came to abrupt ends. James had escaped the suffering, or at least pretended to.

Now he peered back at Cyd's empty husk and reached out a loving hand, Hoping Cyd would grope for him. Cyd reforged his old mask and walked the path he knew he needed to. James' episodes faded, he smiled more, and he told Cyd to stop being so cynical. Cyd was being left behind.

He buried his suffering in laughter and music. When Rebecca… was gone… his mask was broken, and he collapsed into a hollow shell.

"How's Sarah?" Cyd would ask. He always asked now. They rehearsed and performed the perpetual, mundane dialogue of adult friends. Next, they'd surely start talking about the weather.

"She's great, but she still won't stay on bed rest, obsessively nesting. Walking every day trying to get the kid out. She says hi, and she misses you." She meant it, to a point. Cyd thanked him and passed on his love. But he knew why James started asking to meet over coffee, not dinner. Not after last time. Sarah tried to care, but how long could she really be expected to put up with him. James always got too drunk when they were together, and they almost always ended up in a fight. It seemed more and more regressive each time.

The smiles faded. James stared at him for a while. "Twenty-two days. I wonder why." Cyd still liked this about James; at least he never talked like he could fix him. They had been through hypocritical healing conversations already. Everyone else that tried to help said the same bullshit: go to therapy. People who have never felt mental illness, its grip on their hearts and pressure on their brains, have been brainwashed into talk therapy. Cyd was torn on the subject; it had never helped, but there was always some hope that it would. The rise in therapy made people less accountable to each other. It was an easy escape from the inevitably awkward conversation. Was there once a time when people were responsible for listening to and comforting their friends? Now, whenever he breached the topic with a new acquaintance or a colleague or an old companion, they sympathized briefly and told him to talk to someone about it… as if that wasn't what he was doing. It was perversely funny. When you seek help, people help by telling you to seek help elsewhere. But to be fair, the only thing that annoyed Cyd more was when they wanted to do it themselves and offer advice. It was always dumb advice. There was no pleasing him.

When James got better, if he genuinely got better, he tried to drag Cyd, kicking and screaming back into society. His sincerity and efforts rang hollow. It's hard to convince a friend that life isn't as bad as they say when, two years prior, you both complained about others who did the same. After a few heated words and one clumsy fistfight in the strip club parking lot, Cyd and James settled into their friendship's new normal, topical and distant, like any adult friends. James shut up and listened when Cyd talked about his episodes, and Cyd stopped acting like he was more important than James' new family.

"Fifteen days," Cyd repeated. "I don't know. It used to be random, but over the past year, they became more frequent. Then, eventually, more regular. But they were just dreams then; they just started creeping into the day a few months ago, like I said. Why every fifteen days?"

"Any new meds?"

"No, I stopped taking Adderall, but that was mostly to try and sleep better." I haven't been conscious when it happens, so there is no real behavioral concern like schizophrenia or anything. Mostly, I come back to reality after a few seconds with my head on the table and brain fog."

"I don't know, man. It sounds like this may need to be elevated above just Doc Lemure. Might need to go see…"

"Yeah, I know. But I have to put in my time with the talker before I can get a referral to a psych."

"But you've had the same one for like six months now."

"Nah, I left Lemure a month ago. It… just sucks. I'm so tired of them not offering any help, just listening. And they give all those stupid-ass comments, 'Oh wow, you're very intelligent, sounds like you've got a lot going on.' It's just depressing after a while. By the third session, I had run out of stuff to talk about, and he just kept asking probing questions about shit I had already discussed. I'm pretty sure he was just an idiot."

James paused, disappointed but at a loss. "What day are you on?" He asked.

"Five," Cyd replied. "I think."

"Any theories"

"Just the usual. I'm going fucking crazy. Can't find anything to stop it."

"Any more flashbacks?"

Cyd's mind is within the confines of social acceptance, resisting the sudden, powerful urge to crush his coffee mug against a passerby's skull. *Freeze. Eye's up. Eye contact. Hold it.* "No," Cyd says finally. *That cold feeling in my hair yet again. I reach up and scratch away the itching of my skin. Peeling and peeling away to reveal only the rot beneath. Come back. Eyes up, eye contact. James has green-ish eyes. Stay focused. Half-smile. Too much, and he won't believe it. Now talk.* "It's alright, I'll figure it out myself." I hear myself say. *Does he get it? Does it matter? As long as it changes the subject, I guess.*

He smiles and dryly replies, "All I wanted was a Pepsi." There is still that. *We can still manage our half-hearted punk rock references. Brain is blurring. Keep it focused. James' smile fades. Now talk, God damn it.* "Anyway, too much caffeine. I'll get you next time. You good in two weeks?"

*James looks up at me; I must have stood up. When did I do that? I can't feel anything below my hips.* "Maybe. We'll see though… the baby is due." *He's squirming. We talked about this. It's not like he's reminding me of what happened. It's not like it doesn't scream in the center of my brain every moment of every day. But there was no way to avoid it. The more I try to demonstrate that it's not personal, that he deserves to be happy and shouldn't have to hide it, the more it becomes untrue. And the more untrue it is, the more important the lie becomes. The more important the lie is, the more obvious it becomes.* James shifted his eyes upward, only for a moment, off and to the left. He was left-handed, so he was looking for logic; *isn't that the way it works?* Only for a brief moment, until his eyes settled back down and fixed upon Cyd's. His brow furrowed, a tranquil moment of spasm belying the frustration behind his words. He stared at Cyd. *Me, I am Cyd.* And James waited patiently for microseconds for some indicator of a reaction. Cyd felt pain and embarrassment and shame but also a faint glow of care and empathy. 'Poor James, to have to keep putting up with me. I wonder if I was half as committed to his friendship when O was born.'

But that faint glow of happiness for his friend's coming family fed the shame and embarrassment of Cyd's never-ending selfishness and forgetfulness. Shame and fear bring tension. It's a never-ending cycle until something breaks; a friendship, a marriage, a person. *It doesn't really matter, I suppose, but it's coming, and nothing will stop it.* But Sarah had the upper hand. The baby. The marriage would survive, or at least it would last longer than their friendship. Maybe it was just time to say goodbye regardless, to cut ties and go alone again. But he couldn't now, not right after this conversation. *Too obvious.* James wouldn't let it happen. He would pull in harder and get in a fight with Sarah about how he's the only thing Cyd has, and Sarah would scream and put stress on the baby, and the baby didn't deserve that stress. 'That's not even fair, Sarah wouldn't scream. She'd just stomach it and swallow that poisonous frustration, feeding it to the unborn baby. No baby deserves to suffer like that.'

Oh, right, the fucking baby. "Oh yeah, my bad. I'll talk to you in a month or two then." Cyd replies, knowing full well that every forced smile drives them further apart, but like a train crash, he could watch but not stop the inevitable.

"Yeah, call me if you need me, though. I mean it. If you're in trouble, I'm there." He lied. He meant it but lied all the same. He lied to me, and he lied to himself, thinking he could still be there. He had his own shit to take care of now. And that's okay. It's okay.

'What a piece of shit. James, me, the whole lot of us. Everyone in that fucking place. I hate them. All of them.

Take a deep breath. Like always... now keep moving. Fuck that fucking waiter. Fuck James. Fuck, this door is heavy.

'God, I'm so tired of this walk. Two miles back to a place I don't want to be in the first place. What time is it? Three twenty-seven. Late enough for a drink.'

Cyd lit a cigarette and turned left down the sidewalk toward nothing in particular. Just walking, like he so often did, as an alternative to standing still. Walking occupied his mind and kept the more serious creeping thoughts at bay on the periphery of his consciousness. That was the natural beauty of walking in the city. There was enough traffic and renegade bicyclists to give you a pleasant, restorative near-death experience if you let your focus wander too far.

October thirteenth, he thought. No wonder it was finally getting cold. The changing leaves were on full display along the riverbanks; tourists stopped and took pictures at the same spots on the same bridge overlooking the Boston skyline. Clicking away with their five-thousand-dollar cameras to get the same hack photo of their trip to post online with all the others. The grand irony being that optimizing them for the web reduced the quality down to that of any cell phone. But people with money tend to forget about money.

He caught the toe of his sneaker on a loose cobblestone. A brick was expelled from its proper place by an invasive tree root. A quiet rip as he pitched his hands forward to catch himself on his knees. His knee was exposed and starting to bleed. A tear in his last good pair of jeans. At least the school year crowd had thinned out; a few weeks ago, he would have plowed into a herd of families. August to September, the streets flooded with teary-eyed parents unpacking their kids' things from the back of expensive SUVs. College students got younger and younger, hugging their parents and smiling to themselves as they prepared for their debauchery. Soon thereafter, herds of drunk teenagers began to roam the streets, convinced that each night holds a special significance and that the world is a massive, rickety behemoth waiting to be dismantled and improved in their image. Every problem can be solved with a song lyric, and every insecurity can be solved with a drink. We all did it, and we were all equally convinced that we were different. We all moved through it and found our niche in the rickety but reliable system and snickered at the naivete of the younger folks trying to slay the behemoth. We laugh because they don't know this behemoth is what protects us from the void outside. It insulates us from the sensory disruptions of freedom, cold, dark, and hunger. This is the world. He brushed the dirt out of his wound and continued down the road.

Around the corner, Rezard, the houseless man who blended in with the sidewalk on weekdays, groaned as he leaned his usual sign up against a long-disabled phone booth. "Anything helps," it read as he stretched his outstretched palms high into the air, just breaching his fingertips across the shadow of the buildings and warming them in a struggling sunlight. His thick jacket, torn at the elbows and sporting a broken zipper, lifted his t-shirt above the waistline of his jeans. He proudly sported a pair of old Jordans, creased and slightly separated from the heels but still broadcasting a bright yellow swoosh.

An older woman stopped briefly to offer a dollar. "No, thank you, ma'am," he chuckled. "I'm off the clock." She paused, confused, before he laughed and thanked her. Taking the dollar graciously and enjoying a rare moment of human connection.

Across the street, a car horn sounded. A shrill mechanical cry that disturbed the relatively peaceful grinding of city noise. Without breaking stride in black pumps with a grey power suit, a young woman kept talking to her client as she rotated her shoulders to make sure her middle finger stayed directly pointed at the now furious man in his silver sedan. She stowed it away only when she had completely crossed the street.

*And yet, they all breathe. And yet, they all live and die.* Cyd brushed off a half-formed thought about measuring self-worth. 'Without society, how would we know who we are?'

"On your left." A runner skirts by Cyd and picks up the pace, heading toward the Boston skyline. It was ten degrees too cold to run without a shirt on, but that never stopped them.

A brisk wind comes up from the west and nearly blows Cyd's cap off as a flock of Canada geese flutter their way onto the river and kick themselves to shore to look for discarded potato chips and cigarette butts. They gravitate toward the houseless camp underneath the bridge. The camp had been growing but wasn't raided. Cops swing by every now and again to look for drugs or bodies. But they left peacefully. The city did its best. There were services, but no one could cure abuse or addiction. It's a paradox dressed in morality. Alleviating suffering cannot prevent it. In fact, it can help it spread, like a disease that goes unnoticed until it's fatal. Somehow, they managed to keep them from begging everywhere but Harvard Square. At the square, they seemed like a sideshow for the tourists to gawk at. Dirty, middle-aged men in second-hand Nikes holding signs that poked fun at their situation like they were in on some cosmic joke. "Paying off student loans," one would read. He'd laugh and charm the tourists in some perverted show of modern minstrelsy. But around the corner, on the benches off the main walkway, lay the others. The addicts, the schizophrenics, all of the ones that couldn't perform, lay there shouting at God or passed out while the fentanyl slowly squeezes the life from their bodies.

'What was that Huxley quote? The one the Doors were named after?' If we could peer through the doors of perception, we would see the world for what it is, infinite. Or something like that. When we remove that scaffolding, we find ourselves in a black pool. Treading water indefinitely. No value, no change. It's enough to make you suicidal, and it often does. After his own time in college, Cyd peered into that void and had to confront the reality. So many who see the void turn to religion. It's a comforting glow. Protection and knowledge are granted only to those who accept the idea that they cannot understand all.

But faith was a gift that Cyd hadn't been given. He couldn't will himself into believing even when he tried and wanted to so badly. Not even at the end, when he stood on that billboard, he had cracked a rib trying to climb. Staring out at the highway below. He had finished half a bottle of whiskey, determined to work up the courage he had failed to muster so many times before. And he stood in the warm wind, July. Swaying in the breeze and listening to the rushing water noises of the traffic below. How far was it? I think the apartment was five stories? Then they climbed to the roof, then another fifteen to twenty feet up the steel frame to the billboard. Surely fatal. Not like the old science building at school.

Sure, there were lots of tall-ish buildings here. Mostly dorms and apartment buildings. But he was older now; he didn't find himself wandering into the slums and seeing what doors he could open. Access to a roof was once a mark of pride. You'd hear about it during a pre-game for the night's escapades. You'd inevitably end up at some random dude's house with a group of underaged, hammered friends. The dude was inevitably a few years older, always too sober or too drunk for anyone to feel safe. Like a spider waiting for prey. Not now, though. Now, Cyd would be the weird guy with roof access. And no matter how lonely he felt, it seemed a bridge too far. Plus, he'd have to entertain nineteen-year-olds. And that seemed like a lot of work.

But he couldn't jump back then. Not on any roof he found or that billboard, looking down on the interstate from so high. Cyd swayed and cried and tried to jump but couldn't. Just too scared. And as he peered out across the city lights, he saw them extend into infinity. He saw the streets below and, in them, the organized and mindless bustling of ants. He saw red blood cells carrying oxygen through arteries and, at the same time, saw brain cells transmitting electrical impulses off into the distance, carrying information and purpose.

And at that moment, he saw reality for what it was: an infinite system of systems of nodes and connections, hubs and spokes, circles and lines. Everything was at once significant and meaningless. If that was reality, then living or dying did not make a difference. So why go through the pain? Suicide was just some grand theatrical gesture on a stage with no audience, and it left nothing behind but a mess to clean.

So he climbed down, a supreme being, in total conscious understanding of the universe. But it didn't do any good for him. He tried to piece together his thoughts the next morning but remembered only the vision. Everything was connected; everything varied along an infinite spectrum, yet everything was the same. A vision of reality that was at once liberating and terrifying. It created his inner equilibrium, the constant desire to kill himself upon the alter of nihilism against the cold understanding that there was nothing afterward to explore. When nothing is truly nothing, there is no payoff to disrupting the status quo.

He turned into a small dive bar on the corner, one of the last remaining bars in town that wasn't busy pandering to the college crowds. He couldn't help but smile at the familiar face in the mirror behind the liquor bottles. Resisting the urge to twist his unruly beard. It was getting out of hand. Last time, he pulled out enough hairs to see specks of blood pooling to the surface, and he needed it to hide the scars, those shameful trophies of a dozen fights after he lost Becca and Ophie. They painted his cheeks and crooked nose in shameful trophies; the other guys, whoever they were, never quite knew what they were getting into. Sometimes, Cyd forgot he was human. His reflection reminded him that he was a player in the game, whether he liked it or not. He chuckled to himself, wondering how he became such an insufferable jackass. Best not to change now; trying would require admitting that he hoped for something better. But there was nothing better for him. He had used up his happiness and chose to sit back in his suffering with the rest of the destitute and enlightened souls. So he ordered something cheap and put up his hood, trying to discourage any kind-hearted soul that might see his loneliness and try to connect.

# BEAUTY AND SUFFERING

"You promised today was the day." She felt her weight shift to her heels and back toward the sidewalk. It seemed so much scarier in person. No matter how many times she tried, she couldn't get past the distant robotic expressions of the drivers below. Her stomach churned, and she "ah fuck!" One of her gloves slipped out of the tightly mangled bunch of fabric in her hands and drifted to the highway below. Carried by the tumult of the morning commute, that artificial hurricane of cars forcing their way through the morning fog along the interstate. Grim, emotionless people careening through the world, barely cognizant enough to notice the waifish twenty-something woman teetering on the overpass above them, waiting patiently for the impulse to sail through someone's windshield.

If they had looked up, they would have seen nothing extraordinary. Aside from where she was standing, Stacey would have blended into a crowded punk show just as easily as a pretentious café. Her skinny jeans tucked into

"

leather moccasins and a thick coat shielding her shivering body from the fall air. She leaned back and tossed her remaining glove as high into the air as she could. She aimed for the windshield of a semi delivering beer downtown but stumbled backward as the wind pushed her glove back toward her and onto the street behind. It landed in the oily gutter festering with yesterday's rain water. She landed on her back and knocked the wind out of herself. This wasn't a good day.

Stacey paused to cough and wheeze and collect herself. Her head began to throb when she stood up and leaned against the concrete barrier, looking back west along the highway. She sighed. Today wasn't the day. So she grabbed her still-warm coffee neatly placed to the side and continued down the road toward the art gallery.

Stacey always thought she could have been an artist. These city galleries echoed with desperation and… well, echoes. Nothing on the concrete floors, plain, whiter than white walls with haphazard splashes along the floorboards. Nothing to distract you from the art. Curators and artists force themselves upon you, prying for questions, desperate for connection. Art wasn't lucrative until it was. Does she really expect five thousand dollars for a three-color abstract? Maybe it works for them. Initial pricing reflects self-worth more than actual value, and at least anchoring bias is on their side. Do you think the first few people who saw Rothko paint thought he was full of crap? What about Pollock? Did he unveil his creations to a close friend who just humored him too much?

The grey, bustling rush of traffic outside the bay windows reminded all of the patrons that their forays into deeper consciousness were a fleeting mirage. No matter how much they sought connection, the vicious world waited for them outside, both indifferent to their absence and ready to feed upon them once again when they emerged. Why have bay windows at all? Art should be an escape. An isolated room may be more appropriate. But maybe they thought it was classier. To be fair, most art patrons were not escaping the horrors of reality, mostly just rich yuppies with half a brain trying to get something to show off at cocktail parties. It didn't even matter what it was as long as they felt cultured. Shit, the world still talks about Andy Warhol as if pop-art was some revelation and not just cheap bullshit.

Now, the art world is concerned about artificial intelligence. Or, more accurately, people seemed concerned about art. When a computer can generate original work, non-art people suggest that art itself is dead. But Stacey never saw the concern. Art requires sacrifice, and it always has. If it doesn't require sacrifice, it's not art. But no one seemed to see it that way. Maybe it was because she didn't hang out with any artists. Will AI destroy art? Or will it just make it unprofitable again? As it had been for millennia.

Crude cave paintings are art, no matter how crude, or unimaginative, or inaccurate they are. Not because it was the limit of their capability. Humans are genetically identical to the cave-dwellers ten thousand years ago. Cave drawings are art because of the sacrifice. The opportunity cost of spending that time perfecting techniques that would last for thousands of years. They sat in a cave and drew instead of hunting, gathering, breeding, and doing everything else it takes to survive. That time was costly.

Scarcity also increases its value, but what made the art scarce? Usually, the skill of the artist, which had a prohibitive cost to achieve, or perhaps the unique story of the art itself. The moment it represented in history, either of the world or of the artist. Either way, the costs imposed to create and distribute art are what makes it art. In art history class back in college, Stacey was called a cynic because she spoke about art in economic terms. But she believed it was quite the opposite. Cost is value, and we use money to measure that value. Value is desire; art serves no purpose other than to be desired.

In this depressing gallery, artists desperately wanted to connect their creations to people, but most couldn't escape the economic realities of their situation. Unfortunately, that's why all the best art is made by the suffering and destitute, but the only successful living artists are rich enough to focus on art. "The suffering have nothing to lose, and the privileged hold nothing at risk for their craft. To the suffering, art is a means of psychological survival. Only normal people are devoid. They can make a living in the regular world, outside of galleries and studios, but not so much that they can abandon the normal trappings of life voluntarily to focus. Normal people make the worst art. Normal, happy, sober people are the worst of the worst."

"I'm sorry, what was that?"

Stacey jumped and twisted around to see the question-asker. A skinny student, carrying a sketchbook and art history textbook in his left hand, smiling, waiting for his answer. She must have been speaking out loud again. "Nothing, sorry," she muttered, turning away and staring intently at the wall.

The first piece loomed on a glass wall in front of Stacey. It was tall and imposing, stretching nearly from floor to ceiling. Illuminated by a spotlight that couldn't overpower the cacophony of the city on the other side of the big bay windows. The rushing of midday traffic on the bridge outside sought to consume the attention of the patrons, but the piece managed it well. The swirling of black and yellow on a sea of turquoise. Like music dancing over the Caribbean Sea. A calm trickling of melodies that soothed the spirit. It transformed the muffled rush of traffic into the gentle lapping of waves. Stacey felt her face relax and thought briefly of the peaceful life she could never have. This was always the blissful elation of a dive, they briefest weightlessness of flying before the inevitable cold. She felt happy for a second and knew immediately what was coming. And as her psyche hit the waters below, she felt herself shrink.

'Some burdens can never be lifted; they can only be carried.'

And with that trope gouged into her mind, she thought of Sean and the things that killed him. And the peaceful mirage of the painting slipped away, plunging her back into the icy depths she knew so well, which always felt colder after surfacing, even for a moment. The turquoise paint itself seemed to react as a cloud passed over the sun outside, blanketing the world in a grey miasma, and the piece in front of her, a sea-blue. The cascading swirls of black lines were a net cast into the mirky depths. The splotches of yellow were the empty promise of a catch, of survival. No doubt, they would shimmer and disappear when bringing in the harvest, and our stomachs would go empty. Everything was wasted.

"Do you have any questions?" A quite voice leaped out from behind her. Stacey jumped.

It was always painfully awkward to talk to artists. It must be just as bad for them. Art people are weird. Sometimes, the rich wore suits; other times, they wore pajamas. It left all the normal people stuck, having to explain that they aren't going to buy anything. The artist couldn't let some of them be; there was no way to distinguish the buyers from the moochers. "No, thank you," Stacey replied. It made her feel poor. Which was a horrible thought to have. But there was no better word. 'I'll look at all your hard work but won't pay for it,' she thought. She began to move on to the next piece, shuffling away from the greying woman who looked at her now with sincerity, belying her red-cheeked embarrassment. Artists always have to pretend they appreciate the simple admiration of their work, but you can't eat admiration.

"Oh, I didn't mean to disturb you. Please let me know if you have any questions. I'm featured here for the next week." The grey woman sped up as she spoke, taking one step to follow Stacey. But she must have thought better of it as she shrugged her shoulders and turned to walk toward a young couple in business attire.

'Two yuppies at an art gallery on a Tuesday morning instead of at work?' Stacey thought. 'There's your mark' as she moved on. "Thank you, I'll let you know," Stacey replied as she slowly and deliberately backed away as if trying to make sure a floorboard wouldn't creek. *Toe, heel. Toe, heel.* She wondered if she looked like a threatened animal and thought it best to turn around and walk straight to the other side of the room. She skirted on toward the next few pieces and glanced over her shoulder to make sure the woman wasn't following her.

She reached her shaking hands into her purse, digging along the bottom. They grew thinner and bonier; the cold was turning her skin translucent. She bent over and opened her purse in the light, digging through makeup and old gum and a wallet and change and two expired condoms and a quarter of a bag of skittles. Found it. She felt the small light bottle and squirted the last vestiges of alcohol onto her dry hands. Searing pain made her shake more as the chemicals seeped into the tears in her cuticles and under her chewed fingernails. She winced and tossed the empty bottle back into the purse. Holding her hands in front of her with fingers splayed, trying to blow on them to cool the burn. She waved them around through the worst of it, but pushed her glasses up the brim of her nose and concentrated on the tapestry in front of her.

Like most professional artists, this one had found her niche, her preferred technique. Every painter wants to have a "yellow period," one that scholars look back on in admiration, even if they're admiring how terrible your work was compared to other times. That's so many artists' dreams, isn't it? To be so revered after death that high school students stare at their work in agony and try to figure out what the teacher wanted to hear when she asked them to talk about how the picture makes them feel. But perhaps that isn't fair. Motivations are complex. Some paint or sculpt to keep their own demons at bay, to express their agony without using words, or maybe just to make a living outside of an office. Some may just think it's fun. Who knows? This woman, Stacey glanced back again as she shuffled toward the yuppie couple; she had decided that swirls of dark lines on bright backgrounds was her niche. Various hues broke up her otherwise swirling but uniform patterns in ways that may have meant something.

The woman, this shuffling artist, may have been taller in her earlier years but hunched over slightly, doubtless the result of years spent sitting over a canvas. Her light brown hair began to grey elegantly from the roots. It draped over her shoulders and down to her mid-back, nearly covering the silk shawl she wore to accent the thin wool cardigan she wore underneath. A knee-length floral skirt of a dissonant pattern revealed her bare calves and dingy canvas flats that scraped across the floor as she shuffled around. She must have been freezing in this concrete bay. More reason to walk around and talk to people.

She wrung the shawl with her hands, sometimes tugging at both ends like a smarmy businessman tugging his suspender straps, sometimes tying it in a loose knot before untying it, and sometimes she slid it across the nape of her neck like a towel after a shower. She needed to occupy her hands. Whenever she wasn't touching the shawl, her bony hands drifted to cover her face. She must have been aware. She must have been concerned that this was off-putting. In her eyes, she never seemed to listen to what people were asking, instead, only thinking of her hands and what she was doing with them. Sometimes cracking the knuckles, sometimes wringing them together, sometimes massaging the palms, sometimes covering her mouth or crossing her arms. When she caught herself touching her face or biting her nails, she quickly reached down and tugged on the shawl once more. The shawl itself, silk, and covered in patterns of lilacs and tulips and chrysanthemums. It was certainly worse for wear and desperately needed to be cleaned, but the silk was strong, and the wrinkles didn't appear to tear. It was probably her best accessory, a grown-up security blanket. Stacey wondered if that was her only one, a gift from a late lover, or perhaps she stored dozens neatly hung in a walk-in closet. You could never quite tell with artists.

Around the corner of a whitewashed wall. A barrier that separated the two artists featured in today's gallery. It was essential when the artists were so dramatically different. It allowed them to keep their brands pure. A menacing aura loomed in this second room. Stacey noticed before she peaked around the corner. The light itself was darker. The fluorescent bulbs seemed to emit only shadow and whispering fog. A shallow section, walled off from the windowed side. By choice? Stacey wondered. A different sense here. Cold grey pedestals rose from the floor and elevated effigious lumps of plaster and clay. Each artistic transgression was born from the floor. An abomination of figures draped in cement and frozen in time. Each was a rendering of pain and desperate, futile struggle, strong arms and backs dragged down by chains twisting and tortuous knots of bondage debriding the hallowed bodies. Their torture, so profound and menacing that the blackness of their creases seemed dark enough to swallow the world, leaving them impossible to measure in any objective sense. They seemed to heave and sigh with exasperation as their forms flexed rhythmically against the air and light engulfing them. Was the light flickering?

Stacey didn't notice the murals behind them. Massive white canvases with black faces smeared across them. To the unsuspecting eye, the forms were impossible to pull from the viscous and putrid swirls of ink. But Stacey saw them through the Rorschachian illusion. This one, this artist, was a seer. She knew about the terrors. And she knew about him. From the faintest highlights and deep crevasses, Stacey saw the form take shape. The greasy black mane concealing dinner plate eyes and rows of soaked fangs. Next to it sat another with long, sharp claws and menacing power. It was them. Staring down from her as she assuaged the electric pangs of fear that gripped her chest as she first looked up and saw them poised to strike.

She thought of Sean and the things that killed him. The things that would leave so little of him behind. The things that talked through his brain and manipulated him even before the heroin. Her heart slowed, and Stacey glanced around the room. No one. No interested patrons or even polite ones. She felt guilty; everyone was more interested in three-color bullshit. But still, that was no excuse to assault them with this horror. She felt the burn of chaotic anger emerge. Who dared create these things? Who loosed them upon unsuspecting patrons? Stacey looked behind each podium for the culprit who birthed these abominations onto the world. Who was the sighted artist? She expected to find a ragged child, huddled in the fetal position, but found... no one. No artist, no culprit. She was alone with the demons and felt them begin to emerge from the canvas.

*Heel...toe ... heel ... toe.* Stacey crept as if she was stalking prey. She always caught herself walking more quietly when she was nervous. Remnants of her time with Sean, sneaking through the woods. Trying to catch squirrels and birds, cawing like crows to track each other. No one. No one lurked behind the artwork, no one hid behind the curtain in the corner, or in the short hallway to the storage room. These were them. These were the same terrors she saw in her dreams. Stacey, Sean, Adrian, the witness to the eleventh street murder, that guy that disappeared last month. We can't all see the same things by coincidence. There must be more! There is more.

But no one was there. The abominations were birthed alone as if by some Hellmouth, and Stacey began to wonder if she was here today at all to witness them. Perhaps this was another dream or vision or whatever they were. She sighed with despair and relief. She glanced up at the pallid eyes of the beasts. They hungered for her.

And it was there. *Go Down... come find me... I have him... come... go down...*

Stacey turned to leave when she saw her culprit. The greying woman from the far side, she stopped tugging at her shawl, her hands hung limply at her sides. She stared, half hidden from the edge of the barrier. Stacey caught her eye and lingered. Expecting her to duck away or say something, anything. But her gaze lingered. The hollow woman pulled her shawl over her head and tied it tightly around her chin. Her hands covered her nose and mouth like she was about to sneeze, but her eyes locked onto Stacey. Cold eyes filled with deep desperation and fear. They sent frigid pains through her spine, chilling her heart, almost lifeless. Of course, Stacey tried to smile and took some cautious steps toward her. Like she was moving calmly to a cornered animal. And the woman began to shudder. "It's okay," Stacey tried to whisper but instead mouthed weakly. When she got close enough, the two stood silently for a moment. They locked eyes, and Stacey was transported back to a time when her vulnerability and horror were fresh and sour. She remembered the walls of that horrible gymnasium and gawking teens giggling under their breath. She remembered the beheaded girl. The girl that was four pieces levitating above their reality.

She was young then; Sean had just died, she wished it away for years, attributing her waking nightmares to grief and alcohol. She smothered the creeping voice that whispered in the hum of white noise. It mocked her every day. *Maybe you're just crazy.* That wasn't it. *Maybe Sean isn't dead.* No, not quite there. *Maybe you killed Sean.* God damn it, now you're just being ridiculous. *Maybe you should kill someone else, just to be sure you didn't kill Sean.* Yeah, maybe.

Surely she would get déjà vu or something, right? But no, she hadn't killed anyone, she thought. But she fantasized about it more than she cared to admit. But in so many sessions, like now, she wandered off into nothingness and jolted herself back to the present. Locking eyes like so many years ago, waiting for the woman to give a sign of life.

The woman sobbed quietly, her weak lungs straining against her bones. "You see them," she stated… or asked… it was hard to tell. Stacey nodded and paused for seconds and millennia. The two of them were locked in a cycle of pleasure and torture. Like a boy and his distant father, each craving connection but lacking the tools. Their vulnerability walled off from the world. There were no doors to open, so they load up their meaningless sentences with weight and purpose, lobbing them over the walls at each other and hoping the other understands what they really want to say. This was no dream. There is no more painful happiness than being understood. The vindication only shows you that your misery is real.

"Do you hear him?" Stacey asked. The woman's eyes widened, and her pupils contracted, adjusting to the light and leaving her a ghastly, wrinkled thing.

"You should go," she whispered as the tears welled up in her eyes. Her shuddering bordered a seizure now, coming up from her knees into her chest and neck.

"Wait, I'm not here to hurt you. I'm looking for him." Stacey reached out, and the woman withdrew. Her pupils disappeared into the vast sea of her light blue retinas, and she seemed suddenly calm. "I think he killed my brother." Stacey pleaded quietly as the other patrons continued to mill about on the happy side of the wall.

"He did; he consumes all. Everything that we love and hate. Don't look. Maybe you can escape, I thought for a while that maybe I could, but there was nowhere to run-i-couldn't-l e a v e I h a d n o m o n e y s o I t r I e d b o o z e a n d b e f o r e l o n g I w a s s h o o t I n g u p t h r e e o r f o u r t I m e s a d a y a n d o v e r d o s e d t w I c e o n p I l l s a n d c o c a I n e b u t s t I l l n o m a t t e r w h a t t h e r e w a s n o w a y I a l w a y s h e a r d h I m d e e p b e l o w t h e s u r f a c e. He's always there… always." The calm woman's retinas brightened and shook. She coughed and gasped for breath, closing those wide eyes and resting her hands on her knees. Her wrists quivered and seemed to shrink ass she struggled to hold herself up. Stacey suddenly wondered if a strong breeze might push her into a street. Perhaps she lived in this gallery to survive. Was her new frailty the cost of unburdening herself? Or was it a punishment? Stacey felt her chest turn to lead and threaten to pull her to the concrete floor.

The woman gasped again and raised herself, meeting Stacey's gaze with a cold glare and a calm voice that was not her own. It scraped itself along her eardrums like the desperate fingernails of the buried alive. "Of course, go see him. He'll help you; he'll help us all. We just need to find him." As her voice faded, Stacey knew she had lost her and felt the shock of a looming threat. She thought of the paintings behind her and jerked her neck around to see the terrors that loomed to grab her. Were they taller than before?

Nothing, just paintings. The lights that had seemed to fade were suddenly blinding, and she felt the aggressive urge to escape. *Go Down... come find me... I have him... come... go down... I have peace...* Stacey thought and looked back around at the frail woman in front of her. Her pupils had returned, and she stared intently into Stacey's eyes.

"You need to leave now," she said firmly.

Stacey said nothing as she shuffled to the door past the oblivious couples. She pulled the heavy glass against the suction of the outside and emerged into the cacophony of freezing wind and screaming cars. She saw her daydreams, like always briefly considering leaping into the road, but the traffic here was always so congested. No one could move fast enough to make it work. She was ragged, she was torn. She was safe for now. Glancing eastward into the wind, a cold gust rushed in from across the river and knocked the breath out of her. She gasped and heaved and lurched over a nearby fencepost to vomit into the perfectly manicured bushes of a dentist's office. She wiped her lips on her scratchy wool jacket and shuffled to a gas station for a bottle of water. She took the extra time to cross the street before passing the art gallery. She probably wouldn't go back until next week.

# ECHOES AND MISERY

Pain. There is pain. The first thing I feel. Where am I? The pain is below my waist. What is happening? What is my name? Why can't I see? WHY CAN'T I SEE!? It's okay, breathe. Doc says I need to stop getting so worked up. Just… brea…eathe. I can't stop coughing. I can't breathe. What is in my mouth? The wet, chunky warmth of vomit. Okay, the airway is clear; I can breathe. Why can't I see? Are my eyes closed? Oh shit, I'm numb, that's why I can't move. Come on, open your god damn eyes.

Pain again. This time in my left eye. The right seems fine though. A dark grey blur in front of me. But I see light glistening. I'm lying on my left side in some viscous liquid. That explains the warmth and pain in my eye. I see an arm in front of me. Is that mine? No, painted fingernails, it's not me. Where am I? Looking up, I think it's up, the cold serrated lined of steel scaffolding. There is no light but a faint green glow penetrating from the next room.

I have to shift; something has to move, right? Am I still even in my fucking body, or am I just…

What was that? A shift in the air. Not a smell, all I can smell is rot and sour death. Not a sight. Just dark and grey and blur in front of me. And a lone, motionless arm. Splayed out, not moving, scuffed, chipped nails revealing light, summery pink through the holes in the muck. The ring finger sporting a small jewel and some fine pin-striping that may have been tribal or Indian-themed. Whose arm is that? I can't see the base. I can't move my head, just my one good eye down the wrist to the forearm. A small bird tattoo on the inside of the wrist. Maybe a raven? The skin looks young, but it's too dark to tell; all colors except the fluorescent pink are muted by the dim lighting. Past the small raven, staring woefully at the hand, judging the actions of the owner, wrapped a loose sleeve with a button still neatly fastened. The fabric was wispy and fine, like maybe silk? Or some fancy blend. A young woman's business outfit? Dark stains cover the shirt and skin. Is that blood or something else?

Still no movement, my good eye begins to burn as I stare for a sign of life. Am I alone? A shift again. That stir in the air. A vibration so fine it is a bitter taste in the air. At least I can taste now I suppose. If it's a taste at all. Like licking a dying battery or drinking orange juice after brushing your teeth.

I am not alone.

No signs of life, but I am not alone. There is something in here, some ominous threat.

What are you? Lurking, watching. Maybe I should stop trying to move. I'll lay still for a while. Where are you? I feel you in the air. I feel you but I can't see you or hear you or smell you? I can taste your presence, your hunger. Is that for me?

I am not alone. Do you know me? Do you know that I'm alive? Where the fuck are you? What the fuck is going on? Is she dead? Still no movement. The raven stares at her limp hand. I wonder if it feels trapped. If it would suddenly take flight and escape through whatever horrible corridors found them both there.

Down? I am down. I am underground, lying in a closet. In a dark pit without escape.

The room begins to shift. The air moves again. Breathe.

Just… breathe… Just… breathe. In and out. Bring down the heart rate. Control your body.

A shuffle in the room. What's that noise? The wet, insectoid sounds but, too loud, and too heavy. I hear the splash of liquid, a muffled groan.

"uuuuunnnnnn…                    unnnnnooooo…

NOOOOAAAAGH"

God, it's a person! The screams fill the void with echoes muffled by the concrete walls. I hear a clang of metal on metal. And the unmistakable crack of a large bone. The sound still haunts me from my femur break in high school.

I played football! God, the horrible screaming continues. Why can't I move! What was that? A toe? Yes, I felt my toe strain against the inside of a shoe. Am I getting feeling back? I feel pain now, all through my back and right shoulder. But they won't move. It's a good sign, though. Pain means no paralysis right? No, it doesn't;

paralyzed patients often feel intense, never-ending pain. So that's out. I wonder how I know that. God damn, that fucking screaming! The world turns red, and I feel that horrible clatter reverberating in my skull. The screaming enters my crevasses like a snake and tears away at the marrow of my bones. I'm going to go deaf; I know it! WAIT. Paul. That's my name. Okay, what's my last name? Jensen? Jeffries? Jameson? Whatever, not important. Time to move. Time. To. Move.

The scene in front of me begins to shift, moving up and down. I'm doing it. Keep rocking Seth, no. What's my name? Fuck I lost it. It's okay, just keep rocking. I feel the warm black ooze flow into my nostrils, and I cough and spit it out. I smell the rotten air, thick with rust and roadkill.

*Do you think they'll make it?* I saw a face in the darkness. A memory? How recent?

"Fuck no, they won't make it Tobey." I hear a voice say. Mine? "Don't be stupid. She's been dead for hours. You'd need to be fucking Dr. Frankenstein to make this work." Tobey looked across at me from his seat. He was sobbing. "Listen man, what I'm saying is, this isn't on you. There is literally nothing you could have done. They were gone before we even got the call.

Medical equipment lining the walls, but there was such a small room. Not a doctor, an EMT. The room was shaking. I hit my head on a shelf… the back of an ambulance.

"I don't know if I can do this job," he said shakily.

"Hey man, it's not always like this. Most of the time, it's overdoses and administering NARCAN. Other times, it's old people and heart attacks or strokes. Most of the time, they live, and you can go to sleep knowing that you did something good. Eventually, you just get sick and tired of the dramatic crybabies that sprained their ankle, or the anorexic trophy wives that faint because they haven't eaten in days."

"But sometimes it's a fucking baby." Tobey's stupid, teary smile revealed his crooked front tooth.

"Yeah." I forced in a new breath and put my mask back on to protect myself from the growing smell. "Sometimes it is. Life's a bitch, and then you die, we are all going to wind up similar someday. I just wish I could get there before shit like this happens, not after."

"What would you do?"

"I'd kick her right in the fucking chest."

"You don't think she was sick and needed help?"

"Honestly, I don't care. That's why I could never be a doctor or cop. People have always needed help. There have always been traumatized people traumatizing people. But now that we recognize that it's not their fault, that there is no such thing as real evil, we decide that society needs to take on the burden of everyone else. I mean, we're animals; the more people we save that should die, the weaker we become as a species."

"But you save people for a living." His incredulous brow inspects me as I rant.

"Yeah, I do. You caught me; maybe I'm all talk."

"Seriously though… why do it then? Or do you put in less effort on the people that should be dead anyway?"

"I don't think so. I guess I just recognize that I'm not in the position to make that decision. Who knows if I'd be selected for life if someone came across me. Who knows if I deserve it? Maybe it's some way of paying it forward. That's the paradox of medical science, isn't it? As we cure more diseases, as people live longer and longer, death is becoming a choice, and it's a choice no one is willing to make. We are all keeping our loved ones alive in the hopes that someone will fight just as hard for us when we are in that position."

"How is that a paradox?"

"I mean, life would be better for the living if there were fewer people. Less competition for resources, more distribution of wealth. But the living fight to keep the dying alive because they know their time will come."

"Not everyone fights for it."

"Yeah, she certainly didn't. That's why I would have no problem caving in her face if it meant saving the baby. The baby didn't even have a chance to be a bad person yet." The weight of the world shifted as the ambulance rounded the corner into the driveway, and I watched the prepped but idle bag of saline swing toward Tobey at an angle as he looked back down at the scene between us and began to cry.

CLANG! And I'm pulled back to my living reality. A wretched hell of confusion and pain. Different confusion, different pain, but they reside, nonetheless.

"Go down," he had said to me. I remembered the sound. The brain can feel. When he was talking to me, I felt his existence; I felt his malice, and then I felt his comfort and promise. But now, he had forsaken me. He has abandoned me. And in his memory, I hear only the faint and impotent voice. None of the echoing terror, none of the screaming animals. I don't feel the warm light of his tones massaging my cortex, and I don't feel the lingering threat of hell just beyond sight of the darkness. It's just a voice now.

I remember flashes. The haunting of the children burning into my brain and memory, the bloated corpse of a baby girl that followed me home that night and every night to torment me. I felt the shame and terror welling up before he came to me. And I thought I could escape. I could find it. He promised me. I walked. All the way down. And I disappeared. I found myself here. Covered in filth and muck and sin and death, staring at a hand that knew neither life nor death and some fucking bird tattoo that stares at me mockingly.

A shuffle, the soft chittering of a stealthy movement. What was that? Softer now. Clang, clang, clang. It's closer now. Wait, why can I hear it? Fuck. The screaming stopped. When did the screaming stop? Does it see me? How did I not notice the screaming stopped? *Quiet.* I feel it again. Waiting. But it recedes. I can no longer taste the air. I stick out my tongue and feel the muscles in my face begin to shift. I can no longer taste the air. It's not like licking a battery, just warmth. And the smell returns, the toxic, oily, rotten smell that soaks into my skin. If I live, I'll never get it out of my pores. It's a part of me now. Maybe I was the source all along. My skin is rotten.

I rock some more and reach my back. My left eye is useless, but I see the dark, geometric patterns of brick or cinderblock along the walls and ceiling. Any glints of light are starred and scattered in my field of vision. I see a small catwalk above me carrying conduit wires and some thin piping. I see the imaginary orange of rusted steel in the dark. How much of this is real? How much am I making up? And I see flashes of a horrible face. Days ago, or decades ago? The tiny, swollen blue-grey face, the flesh beginning to swell and bruise. The acrid, sour smell of vomit and shit.

The CLANG! Another visitor. It's inside the room. But where? I shift my head to the left. The grey, hopeless outlines of bricks and stone emerge from the black. Maybe my good eye is adjusting. Or perhaps I'm just paying attention; terror can blind you. Funny how adrenaline can make your vision either incredibly clear or completely opaque. I've always wondered about the limits of our senses. At what point is our reality just subjective. Are there any objective parts at all? Still turning to the left. I see faint outlines extending beyond the rough cut of the brickwork. Pipes, either electrical or plumbing, bolted to the walls of this little prison. Running off into the distance and into the black abyss of the tunnel that now stretched out before me. I can feel the control returning to my neck, my traps, my brow. Carefully now.

I feel it breathing. How much of our senses are unconscious? Subtle changes in air pressure, rhythmic breathing patterns are all but drowned out by white noise. Sensory triggers that never rise above the threshold of consciousness. Does that count?

Time to check the right side. I can move faster now, but probably shouldn't. I feel it. That rhythmic breathing, almost a gasp. It's weak but close. I can hear it now from my right ear. Silent, but closer. God damn, this thing is sneaky. I slowly pivot my head. No sounds. Don't make a sound. It's so quiet I can't tell if that rushing is the heaving death watching me or just the blood pushing through my ears. It's closer still and creeping along. I feel the air vibrate with its presence. No wonder people get obsessed with things like ESP and sixth senses and third eyes and whatnot. It's definitely here. It knows I'm here. But hopefully, it's more focused on the owner of that goddamn arm and raven next to me. I hear my neck crack and a shiver goes down my spine. Silence, pure silence. No breathing. No pattering feet, no vibrating air. It heard me. It knows I'm here. It skulks in the darkness and approaches its prey.

So quietly… how can something real be this quiet?

My peripheral finally crests the other side, and there it is, hunched and staring. Eyes wide and round, and black to see in the intense dark, twice the size of a human hand. It has long, slender arms reaching out gently, placing jagged clawlike hands on the soft and quiet floor. The pale gray skin traced along a rail-thin skeletal structure down to the long, sharp claws; each must be at least eight inches long. How is it so quiet? It must know I'm helpless. Unless it's not hiding from me. I still can't move. I think it knows. It's creeping forward. Creeping mercilessly. Its eyes meet mine. There's death in those eyes, and based on my current state, It's probably mine. Why does it look so thin? Why does it move so slowly? It's hiding from something, but not me.

CLANG!

The sound is closer, but my creeping stalker is not the cause. Wait, did he just hesitate? The long, exposed fangs emerging from an angular face prevent any facial expression, but regardless, he stopped. He shifted his bodyweight onto his hind legs as if prepared to turn back and run. What in hell is Death afraid of? At that moment, for the first time, his eyes shift away from me, and he searches the room. But he can't see what I see. The new terror that scuttled silently along the catwalk above, perching over us, assessing. No, stalking.

I hope he's coming for the hunched one. Yes, it leans toward the intruder. Pouncing from the height with a fast and heavy thud, he will drive him off. Slashing wildly with its long claw and hacking away. No shrieks, instead a flurry of hollow gurgles and squeaks and clicks of furry and terror. He is distracted, and I'm safe. I let my body relax for a moment and pray that they just move on.

CLANG!

I startle and feel my body seize with the sudden jolt of complacency shattered. Shit. Neither of them made that sound. I see movement above me and know I'm dead. It's smarter than I hoped. Another thick-skinned one beats his long claw on a metal pole. Staring intently at the heap of bodies for signs of movement. I played right into it, jerking my head to the left and broadcasting my life and my vulnerability. A meager head tilt, the closest thing I could manage for a startle response. He sees me now. Hopefully, he gets distracted.

But he is staring right at me, and this time, he knows. God, you fucked up Pete, or Paul, or whatever the fuck your name is. And now he's coming for you, stepping over the heaps of twisted flesh, victims far more spoiled than me, far less delicious. Don't cry, Patrick, just stare at that fucking raven and try to play dead. God, I wish I could just fly away.

But I can feel, I can move, and it has what it came for. The terror has forgotten me, now is my chance. I am screaming now, but I can't hear myself through the lightning in my brain. I know I'm screaming because I feel the pain of my ribcage. It's sharp but muffled under the bone pain I feel shivering through me. The air is passing through my throat and out onto the terror. It knows I'm alive, and it knows I am food. All hope is lost. All the world is silent. I hear only ringing and muffled screams.

But I feel my body, my rotten body, is mostly whole and full of life and energy and will to fight. I feel my toes and my broken rib and my sore throat and the electrifying torture of my arm that spills blood on the walls as I flail, screaming in agony. I have to run. I have to get away now.

I am standing now; I don't know when I stood up or if I was heaved. But I'm on my feet and running. Sharp, searing razors as I run away toward the faint grey light. I think it's chasing me. The thing, not the light. The light itself seems only more elusive as I sprint. It dangles ever further down, reflecting off the gray doom walls. I'm limping and dragging my foot behind me. There is no escape. I have to move. It scuttles behind me, slashing and stabbing as I fight toward the light. Slower and slower. Left, then right, then left. I fall and cough up blood, swallow dirt, and try to find the light. Must find the light.

The moon peeks at me through a storm drain above me. Heavy steel grating cemented into place and just out of reach. I'm blind. The pale glint of the hopeless sky bright beyond comprehension. I imagine the colors swirling throughout time and space, nebulae spanning incomprehensible distances. So spread out that each picture on that wall of my astronomy teacher's office showed a flat image spanning hundreds of thousands of years as the deepest colors took so much longer to arrive. I think of the colors I'll never see, and I want to cry. I am grey, trudging in a world of shit and pain. Black masses in the sky sweep over the moon and close off the last reminder that life exists. Putrid, oily rain spills through the drain and into my eyes. The rushing water of the storm rages at my feet, blocking my path, and death lurches behind me. This must be how the rabbit feels. Mind racing for a solution that never existed.

It knows I'm alive, it knows I'm food, it knows I'm weak, and it knows I've lost. I turn and see it chitter its mandibles with glee and skulk itself into my last little doomed chamber. The clicking and thudding slows as the terror gets closer. There it is now, gleeful at the end of its chase. I almost had him, but I have nowhere to go now. It's cautious; maybe it's not used to standing prey. It stops just out of the reach of my good arm and stretches its claw low, going for my ankle. I weakly kick it away, but it's fast. It reaches and strains and takes hold; ever so gently, it pins me. It raises its long claw, swinging widely, and I see my organs burst from the expanding hole in my gut. The shimmering beauty of the night sky fills my vision, and I say a quick prayer for death. My weight shifts, and I watch my legs stay ashore as I fall into the rushing water below.

# MIRRORS AND MOUNTAIN PEAKS

The common peer into infinity
seeing only what lies before them.
A leader peers for longer
and sees through the void to points of light.
But at the fringe lie the sighted
who peer beyond and fight oblivion.
To accept the pure reality of existence
is to be overpowered by its enormity.
Beating your head against a paradox
until it unravels into string.

*--From the margins of Stacey Travers' Notebook, recovered from her home.*

When Mr. Vickars, the sophomore English teacher, hung himself, the school shut down. Cyd thought, maybe this is what made him sad.

Such an angry kid with no apparent cause. He started drinking at thirteen, sneaking alcohol from liquor cabinets and bars at family reunions. Bright, so clever. "I told you he was going to be president one day," his parents would brag to their friends. Who would smile in admiration and love. So much love from all directions. What was he so angry about?

"You're that one that's going to make it out," they told him. Slowly separating and secluding him until he only found solace in books, and video games, and booze. First, he accepted being alone. Then he enjoyed it. Then he cherished it, all the while hating it. His new schools had longer vacations and more homework. He sought pride in who he was but envied his old life, his old friends. He struggled with connecting, obsessing when a girl was interested, only to detest her for her interest in horoscopes or the way she laughed. Guys were always too violent or not violent enough. He hated people for trying to reach him and hated them more for giving up.

At sixteen, he felt broken. His mind was a prison he never could escape. So he battered the cage, punching walls until his hands bled, shaving his head and piercing his face and between his fingers. He lashed out socially, becoming a performer and a debater and aggressively causing a scene at every opportunity. Desperately wanting to break the rules but crippled by the fear of getting caught. He always removed the piercings, he never cut where he couldn't cover. Desperate for attention but addicted to his brooding and quiet solitude.

When Mr. Vickars hung himself in the swim team locker room, the school shut down. Cyd thought maybe this was what made him sad. Maybe now he had an excuse to be unhappy.

"Why the swim locker room? One kid asked in a hushed tone in the student lounge.

Cyd heard his reply but couldn't stop himself; maybe it was a cry for help. No one answered. "Why not? It's got big, exposed beams that can hold your weight. You can climb up from the lockers, so you don't have to find something to stand on. And honestly, he probably didn't want to be found by his kids. They're too young to go down there." He felt the eyes shift to him. No one said it then, just silence and agreement. Always silence.

"Two hours later, Brandon put his arm around him. "Cyd, you should probably go see someone. You're off."

"What do you mean?"

"You've been standing here starting at that window for six minutes. Are you okay?"

"Oh really?" Cyd half chuckled. "Yeah, thanks, man. I'm good." He pushed off and walked away with a smile that felt like a gaping wound.

Mr. Vickars decided to hang himself with an extension cord. Cyd had always thought that hanging seemed like a bad way to go. He had always had a thing for heights instead. At least with enough of a height, you died suddenly and chocked full of adrenaline. The lock to the roof of the science building was in bad shape. The little plate holding the door mechanism was loose and damaged. It only took a pocketknife to get the last few screws off and open the door to the outside.

It was called the Love Science Center after whatever rich prick alumnus gave the most money for it. It was under construction, twenty million dollars to build they said. Who knew if it was true? What did the kids know about construction budgets anyway? Cyd didn't know, but it was all they talked about. Is that even a lot of money for a building? It's tall, curved brick walls flowed across the sloping grass, ominously surveying the fields below. The dissonance of the tightly organized bricks and fluid silhouette on the horizon drew him in the first time. He crept along the outer fence after hours, lying to his parents about a party at some friend's house. A quick climb, a small tear on the crotch of his jeans that snagged on the sharp points of the chain link fence.

The coarse scraping of the tilled dirt and the hobbit smell of exposed roots suffocating in the cool night air. The inside of the fence was forbidden, and to the flora, a killing field. He checked his balls for blood but couldn't distinguish any colors in the dark shadow of the castle he approached. At least it felt dry, with no sharp pangs when he slid his hand past his belt. He padded his footsteps enough to avoid the echo, not quiet knowing what he was stalking. But entered the maze of rafters and power tools and pallets of wood. Working his way upward until he sweated up the final flight of stairs to find the door that led to the roof. There was no lock yet. Why would there be?

When Mr. Vickars, the sophomore English teacher, hung himself in the swim team locker room, the school shut down. Cyd found him and watched him swing for a few minutes, wondering if there was extra rope lying around and if the beam would hold two. He had wandered into the swim team locker room to climb up and hang onto the beams. He wanted to know if they'd support his weight. But there was no rope in the locker room. All he could find was the power cable of the floor buffer in the down-the-hall janitor's closet. Which was too heavy to carry, and he didn't have anything to cut it.

Mr. Vickars body was still swinging, but barely. So slightly that one wondered if it was just the Coriolis effect. Is anything ever perfectly still? Cyd thought briefly about taking his body down. Mr. Vickars had brought his own extension cord. People would probably get suspicious if they saw him walking along to the gym with a coil of rope. Who is just carrying rope around? Only people looking to hang themselves and, maybe, sailors? And God forbid you get the wrong kind, and it snaps on you. Leaving you very much alive but now with a broken ankle from the concrete floor that you'd have to explain to your family and coworkers. An extension cord was smarter, but that wasn't something a teenager just had lying around.

Two days later, at the top of the Love Science Center, Cyd took a deep breath of the fall air. It carried the earthen smells of decaying leaves and fresh soil up from the river at the edge of campus. A brisk October gust of wind cut through to the bone, reminding him how frail and small he was. Maybe that's why he couldn't bring himself to do it, why he stood there for hours last week. He just paused, staring over the edge to the parquet brick walkways below. Trying to work up the courage to lean a little farther forward, but he never could. So he just thought about the pain. The cold touching his soul and causing spastic shivers,

The funniest thing about suicidal ideation is the dissociation. He always felt the least emotion when we was closest to following through. A separation from his humanity. As he grew increasingly numb, he fantasized more and more about killing himself. It was a thing to do, an insufferable paradox that you had to suffer, and do it alone.

Somehow, that cold, that discomfort of the dead wind clawing through his clothes and onto his flesh, sending shockwaves through his spine, stopped him. Cyd just couldn't help but feel human. Small, helpless, and uncomfortable. Could he really claim to want escape when the slightest cold turned his thoughts to the pleasures of warm blankets and hot coffee? Each time he stood on the edge of that building, he felt alive, and suddenly, the costs of his decisions paraded themselves across his consciousness. Each time, he climbed back down and replaced the locking panel, feeling like a poser.

He was always careful to replace the lock when he came back down. If they find out it's broken, they might fix it. Like sitting near an exit in a crowded theater, knowing that you can leave at any time. Having an escape plan made him feel in control.

After Mr. whatshisname hung himself, it seemed like the right time. Maybe, he thought, someone would take him seriously now that he found a dead teacher hanging from the rafters of the pool locker room, just as he was thinking about the same thing. Maybe they wouldn't just think he was a whiny teenager. Therapy was super trendy these days.

He told his dad on the way home after school. "I think I want to see someone. To talk about things." Even the words hung awkwardly in the air when they escaped his lungs. Weights compressed his chest, making every gasp an effort.

His father shrugged, not a glance to the side. "Okay." the neutrality of his tone stinging. The matter-of-fact support Cyd enjoyed once again rising from his psyche. What right did he have complaining? People are raped, tortured, and murdered every day. Including today. What could he possibly have to talk about? He immediately regretted asking. And wanted to take it back. But taking it back would mean admitting he was anxious, admitting that it was actually important. So he sat silently, listening to the radio that hovered just below the volume of comprehension. News. Something about venture capital. Something about Libya. Something about traffic.

∞ ∞ ∞

The therapist's office was clean, neatly appointed, boringly decorated, and oddly comfortable but at the same time painfully awkward, and Cyd hated it.

The magazines were up to date. Not even having the decency to live up to the stereotype he wanted to complain about. It was so silent the carpets screamed against the shuffling sneakers and cudgels of oxfords and wedges. Every breath was carefully controlled to avoid attracting attention. They all had to pretend they weren't there for the same reasons, like running into a coworker at a porn theater. You have to pretend to be confused and lost. Like you have no idea how you got there.

He sat in the office chair in the stale waiting room. Minutes, hours. Not making eye contact, looking at the ground. His back was aching from slouching, but he couldn't walk around. No one else was walking around. He thought about escaping. About just walking out. Hanging out in the parking lot until his mom came to pick him up. But he didn't know how insurance worked. Would that cost them money? Would they find out? And either way, there was a 50/50 chance she was just waiting in the parking lot. She took these opportunities for micro-naps whenever she could, always stressing about him since the neighbor's daughter killed herself a few years ago. Her anxiety channeled itself into a near-obsessive study of mental health in teenagers. She was so supportive and so obviously and deliberately not smothering. It must have been a lot of work because she had been exhausted ever since. He sometimes heard her walk by his room at night, pausing as if trying to sense if he was alive through the door. But she never checked; she desperately wanted him to have his privacy. Today was only an hour appointment, and the first time he saw a therapist, she would likely stay out of fear that he'd come out sobbing and have nowhere warm to dry his tears.

A light tap on his shoulder. "Are you Cydnie Devins?"

A young woman smiled at him, closer to his age than his embarrassment dared guess. And he watched the room float around him as his numb legs propelled him across the floor and through a heavy wooden door into the yellow-lit hallway.

It wasn't a hospital, and it forced that fact upon him. Everything seemed so deliberately placed in antithesis to a hospital that it made the similarities all the more obvious just below the surface. Cheap paintings and vibrant, fresh flowers lining the walls on rickety antique wall units. They probably swap out flowers too often. Just to make sure they are freshly cut every day. Where do the discarded bouquets wind up? Do they just throw them out? Do they have a dumpster out back full of murdered flowers in various states of decay? What must it be like to be a conscious flower? A life of reaching for the sun, competing for energy to grow bright and beautiful, only to be severed at the base and left on display to die slowly. People ogling at your physical form while feeding you just enough to maximize your suffering. Is it better to be the loser? Edged out of the sunlight, weak and hungry, but never desired. Never targeted.

The carpet had intricate designs, but not for art, just for cleanliness. The kind of swirling circular pattern that tells you this carpet is made for somewhere with a considerable risk of spilled coffee. Maybe occasional vomit or blood. But this wasn't a psyche ward or a prison. It was just a therapist's office. Wasn't it filled with friendly people who just wanted to help others? They certainly went out of their way to make it look that way.

The ceiling gave away the building's age. Everything else was decorated and designed to look somewhat timeless. It was hard to tell if this was from the seventies or the nineties. But the ceiling was plain white sheet rock painted over. Faint dark circles showed where they had tried to hide a water leak. In the corner, the paint peeled up like rusted steel, exposing the dark grey paper covering the drywall below. The drywall never yearned to escape; it remained in form and flat. But the paint itself flawed at the presence of rusty water, as if dying to expose the problems below, only to be met with the vain indifference of the outside world at the sight of the problem.

The door did not lie at the end of a faded hallway, foreboding the end of the line. A simple set of offices that were likely bedrooms when this building was stood up. The first door on the left was closed with a sign reading "Welcome!" His door, the only open one, stood halfway down on the right, with the faint glow of incandescent lights illuminating the wall on the opposite side.

But Cyd paused. No mirrors. That's what was odd. With the rest of the decor, you would expect a large mirror in the waiting room or hallway. It just felt off not to have one. Did mirrors induce shame? Did they scare off patients? Do people feel judged? This was a house without mirrors. No opportunities to look into your eyes and take stock of who you are and where you belong. That, after all, was their job. "Bastards," Cyd thought to himself.

Down the hall and to the right. The young woman told him, and he floated on the short, bristly carpet past the pretentious flowers and turned into the room with the sickening yellow glow. But there was no therapist. Did he want to make a dramatic entrance? Was there more waiting? Maybe he ran multiple rooms like any other doctor. Cyd stood behind the thick couch, unlike the leather Freud couches he had secretly hoped for.

"Go ahead, grab a seat." the young woman told him as she rounded the couch and began to sit down.

Cyd felt his legs again, and it was agony. A weight passed from his chest to his toes, spikes scraped along his bones from his spine into his pelvis, tearing out his femoral arteries and exposing the soft pink marrow of his femur. Not only was he whining about his feelings, but he was a sexist, too. What was worse? Of course she was the therapist, jackass. They don't have nurses.

He felt it, the creeping smile dawning over his face. His mask was back on, and it painted the shell of his body with a thin veneer that she would never penetrate.

"Of course. Thank you." He heard himself say. "How are you?"

"I'm well, how are you?" she asked instinctively.

"I'm fine, thank you." He was fine; there was no reason for him to be here. "Well, not fine, I guess," he chuckled, fake and nervous. He couldn't break free from his gilded veneer, shielding him from connection. "That's why I'm here, I guess." He still didn't sit down until she took her spot on the armchair next to him.

"That's alright, let's chat. Why don't we start with what made you decide to meet with someone, and maybe, if you know, what you are hoping to get out of therapy."

∞ ∞ ∞

An hour later, an eternity later, he stepped out into the parking lot, watching the orange glow of the sun peak out below the day's storm clouds along the horizon. He paused and put his head down, scraping his sneakers along the pavement as he shuffled to his mom's car. She was reading a magazine but had dozed off at some point. He tried not to startle her awake when he knocked lightly on the passenger side window. He was never successful, and she jumped in her chair before unlocking the door.

"How did it go? I'm not asking what you talked about, just if it was good." His mother shifted the car into reverse and her bones creaked as she turned to look out the back window.

"Fine."

Cyd hated himself. He had a pleasant conversation. He smiled and was charming and talked about school. About his good grades, about the few close friends he had. The mask had taken over.

He couldn't stop it. When she tried to get serious. He qualified everything. "I just, want it to stop... but I get it, people are suffering everywhere."

"Yes, they are." She replied. "But that doesn't mean you aren't suffering also."

"Yeah, I'm fine though."

He walked out feeling like a waste of time. His time and hers. He saw the pale orange glow of the sunset radiating from the west over the tree-covered hills of his hometown and knew "there is no escape." He muttered to himself. You'll never escape the pit when your own mind won't let you crawl out.

So he sat back in the passenger seat of the car as they sailed through small-town highways, passing the rows of barren trees and leaning his head against the cold window. He closed his eyes, pretending to be asleep, and thought about how desperately he needed to pull his winter coat out from the back of his closet. Maybe if he was warmer next time at the science center, he'd have the courage to lean further forward. He wondered if three stories on that parquet brick walkway was enough to kill him. He'd probably have to go headfirst. Weird that he had often thought about it but had never heard of anyone successfully jumping headfirst to their deaths. Maybe he should find a higher building.

When Mr. Vickars hung himself in the swim team locker room, did he think about the pain he was causing? Or did he only think of the pain he was escaping? Maybe the extension cord was the answer; was it for an open casket? Did he have that much consideration for his family that he would want an open casket? He chose the swim team locker room because his two kids were too young to go in there. Was he trying to spare them having to find their dad swinging but motionless? Cyd wondered if he had thought about who would find him, or if they would be so ironically bound as having skulked along into the locker room for the same purpose. Mr. Vickars had just beat him to it.

# CHAOS OR COMPLEXITY

Equilibrium doesn't find itself through supernatural means. In school, teachers often speak in terms of a system "wanting" or "pushing" to reach equilibrium. This is a fallacy and a mischaracterization of the relationship between cause and effect. For relationships, they are. Not rules; there are no rules in the way that we think of them. Even laws of physics are broken, and exceptions are possible, but the relationships between nodes, whether we as humans have defined and categorized them or not, exist in spite of us.

There exists also a misconception that equilibrium is peaceful. That it represents a calm after or in between upheavals. But we perceive reality relative to the scale of our point of view. The sun, peaceful and warm, from your seat on the lawn, is an ever-changing hellscape of superheated plasma churning at the surface. The surface itself is an illusion made by the point at which the density of the star allows visible light to escape. Nuclear fusion provides a source of energy pushing matter outward in all directions, trying to force the sun to explode outward into infinity. But gravity provides a balancing loop, pushing all of the matter together, attempting to compress it into an infinitely small black hole. And as these to forces battle for billions of years, they reach a steady state of aggregate, chaotic, and destructive equilibrium that we perceive as a pleasant morning while we mow the grass.

This same dynamic applies to human activity, to all activity. Biological concepts such as punctuated equilibrium translate to military history. The Napoleonic wars were a series of French victories followed by uneasy peace while the continental armies gathered coalitions and prepared for another go. The same can be said for the interwar period. While the allied powers turned inward to nurse themselves and celebrate peace, Adolf Hitler consolidated power and prepared for his invasions.

So, is peace the equilibrium? Or is war? The equilibrium is the complex adaptive system of nation-states that are constantly fluctuating on a continuum of peace and war. Unfortunately, humans are limited by their own cognitive abilities to perceive the infinite. Even limitations so fundamental as our perception of time prevent us from perceiving the true, infinite nature of the universe, or multiverse, or whatever else we have yet to conceive. Humans must, therefore, establish limiting frameworks that allow us to traverse this infinite space. Just as a ladder allows us to travel upward but inhibits our ability to move laterally, the characteristics and study of system dynamics allow us to peek into the infinite soup of interacting variables and fish out insights that we can apply to our daily, three-dimensional world.

System dynamics is founded upon the nature of a relationship between two variables. Relationships are often characterized as either reinforcing or balancing. A reinforcing relationship is one in which an increase in variable A results in an increase in variable B. On the contrary, a balancing relationship is one in which an increase in variable A results in a decrease in variable B. By starting with the relationship, not the variables, this branch of math opens the doors to invent new ways of looking at complicated systems. We hold the interaction of agents for granted and instead invent and discover new variables, new interactions, and new frameworks for perceiving the universe.

To illustrate this, consider an argument between a parent and child. The parent wants the child to obey the rules. To increase compliance with the rules, they discipline the child either verbally or with restrictions (i.e., more rules). But with this particular child, an increase in punishment leads to a rise in rebelliousness, which leads to a decrease in rule-following, which leads to an increase in punishment. This is a reinforcing loop. One that will spiral into infinity unless there is something to balance it out. If there is nothing to counter this cycle, the parent's punishments may increase to the point of physical and emotional abuse. The child's rebelliousness may grow to the point of running away or murdering the parent.

Consider a common example of the relative populations of predators and prey. Imagine a forest populated by wolves (predators) and sheep (prey). The wolves must eat the sheep to survive and reproduce. The sheep reproduce at a constant rate. In this simplified example of an ecosystem, the wolves have no natural predators but will starve to death if they go too long without food. The Sheep reproduce at a constant rate and have an unlimited supply of food. Without the wolves, the sheep would have a reinforcing loop that would spiral into infinity. Their population would never stop growing. But, when you introduce the wolf to a crowded ecosystem of sheep, he can find food easily, has plenty of energy, and reproduces often.

As the wolf population increases, the sheep population declines until there is no longer enough food to do around. The wolf population balances the sheep, and the sheep population balances the wolves. When there are too many wolves, the sheep become so rare that they wolves begin to starve until the sheep population can recover.

This system can achieve an equilibrium if conditions are met (reproduction rates, encounter rates, etc.) that allow the sheep and wolf populations to balance each other indefinitely. However, if a single variable is introduced or adjusted, the system reaches a tipping point and is destroyed. For example, what if climate change enables a blight that kills the sheep's food source? What if a competing predator begins to hunt the sheep? The equilibrium is controlled by death. But if the last sheep die and there is no more, the forest becomes a barren, lifeless wasteland.

These relationships, the foundation of complexity theory and system dynamics, are both enlightening and horrifying. To see the relationship between variables is to see existence for what it truly is, math and death. You can understand the infinite nature of the universe only to fallow at the inconsequentiality of human existence. Any purpose or meaning you might have had often appears to be just the human brain's attempt to grapple with its own worthlessness. Perhaps suicide is the balancing loop against the human mind's incessant need to peer beyond its capabilities into the void.

*-- Excerpt from essay for Prof. Sadiq Malik's "Introduction to Complex Adaptive Systems."*

∞ ∞ ∞

"C-minus? Really?" Harriet's indignance shined through her attempts to mask it. She stared across the table at Sam's chubby face. She had asked to meet up with him again. Her grades continued to slip, and she couldn't afford anything less than a B in System Dynamics if she wanted to do her independent study next year. Her voice was raspy but not muted. Whispering was beyond her emotional range at the moment. She had deliberately asked to meet Sam, Dr. Malik's teaching assistant, in a coffee shop, so she wouldn't just yell at him. It was working so far. Sort of.

"I don't control the grades," he replied, briefly shrugging his shoulders and running his hands through his dark hair. The crisp faded sides and forearm tattoos peaking from under Sam's pink collared shirt belied his time in the military. He had tried to reassimilate back into society with longer hair and a few extra pounds, but Harriet always got the sense that he was more aware than he let on. He leaned back in his chair, and his eyes avoided hers, following a new customer who had walked in through the door behind her.

"Bullshit. Yes, you do. Everyone knows that Malik doesn't do shit outside of lecture."

"Alright, fine, I graded it, but I can only do so much," Sam spoke up, now resolved and defensive. Exactly what Harriet did not want. "Harriet, this is exactly what we talked about during office hours on Saturday, and, if I recall, I told you not to go this route. I understand your theory, and the presentation is artistic, but this is a math class at its core. We are not here to connect the physical and metaphysical through the lens of your opinions on the human condition! We are here to study system dynamics as a means to model and draw conclusions from complex systems. We work within limited, specific professional definitions and while these may seem limiting to you, this is a technical skill."

"Yeah, but you said…"

"It should have been an F… "In fact, it was a fucking F when Malik reviewed it. Which he very much fucking does." He was clenching his left fist now and staring her in the eyes. The clatter of coffee shop banter and colliding dishware kept too much attention off them. "I was able to talk him up to a D before I put in the grades as a C-minus. He may not do the grades, but he will notice if you are suddenly his star pupil. Do you know how few students he knows by name? Well, you're one of them."

"But it's too low. We talked about this when I agreed to… we had a deal." She started. He was not going to renege now. She couldn't let him.

"First off, you threw yourself at me; let's not pretend I solicited. And before you think about going to the dean with accusations, remember you have a history of behavioral problems at this university and that I have never been openly accused of any wrongdoing." When your grades are that bad, do you think that anyone will believe you or care? It's not like I'm artificially decreasing your grades."

"But you're artificially increasing them."

"I get what you're trying to do, but you have just as much to lose as I do, and you know it. Threats aren't going to get you anywhere. I'm not a professor; I technically don't have the authority to input the grades anyway. You may notice I'm not threatening you right now like you are. I am not deliberately lowering your grades. That seems like a clever way to get caught. But you have to give me something to work with. Your paper was garbage, and you know it. You didn't even meet the length requirements."

Harriet paused. "So, what's the solution? It's too low. What can you do?"

Sam softened and let out a sigh. "This is a significant departure from the course material, and we can't magic it away again with another one-on-one session. The first midterm at least looked like you tried, so I could up that to a B-plus. This one though… you need to cut all the philosophical shit. Keep it in creative writing."

"Okay."

"The best we can probably hope for is a letter-grade improvement with some significant re-writes. I'll set aside some time for you this Friday at my apartment to review."

"Can't you just write it?" She asked. Trying her best to appear coy.

"No, absolutely not," Sam replied quickly and flatly, feeling her hand on his knee under the table. "Hey, I get it, but like I said, this is transactional. You don't get more just because you ask nicely." Harriet leaned back and looked up at the shadow in the corner. Sam took a sip from his coffee before he spoke again. "Why are you here?"

"If I have to retake a complexity class, I can't do my independent study next year," she replied lowly.

"No, I mean at MIT," he continued. "I know you're smart, but your writing shows you want nothing to do with the normal, dry research route. I mean, it's MIT; you had to know this was what you were getting into. If you wanted something softer and more liberal-artsy, why not Harvard, or Tufts, or BU or something? I mean, the hardest part about Harvard is getting in. Everyone knows that. You could have shown up and written about your feelings and walked away with an A- in most classes. But you didn't fall in here or accidentally wind up in this program. It took a lot of work, for years. So why are you so surprised that this is what is expected of you?"

Harriet stared intently at the shadow in the corner, watching it deepen and shudder against the sounds of the insufferable meat sacks clogging up the room around her. "It's what I thought I wanted. I wanted to find a reason for all of this. I wanted to find that secret vault of knowledge that explained everything. But it's not here."

Sam stared intently at her face and watched the lines deepen. "What do you mean?"

"You wouldn't understand. And it's not your fault. You're smart, too. It's just I knew about this all before. I found this information during late nights alone in high school. I saw the way we all interact; I saw how mundane we all are, how similar to ants. And the thought is repulsive to most. Why can't anyone else see what I see? I thought maybe studying complexity here would help explain. But all anyone wants to talk about is supply chains and weather patterns. No one wants to talk about the meta-complexity. About the way in which our minds influence the way we perceive, build, and participate in these systems, and about the parallel enormity and insignificance of all of our actions. So, all I want to do is finish this course and keep working on my dissertation. That's all I want to do next year, but I can't if I have to retake this course."

"Well then, put in the effort," Sam said softly. "Maybe you can ask Malik for extra credit if you go straight to him and explain the situation. Then, actually focus on this course. You're not an idiot."

Harriet snapped her eyes back to Sam and put her mask back on. She smiled. "Or… what if I bring a friend on Friday?" She asked and winked. "I have someone in mind. It's like you said, this is transactional."

Sam sighed and leaned back in his chair, running his fingers past his glasses through his long, curly hair. "Would I have to re-write her paper too?"

# ADRIAN'S ESCAPE

After four years of practicing therapy, Adrian was convinced nothing was ever as bad as it seemed. However, this was a tough mantra to repeat in the muck of the Chesapeake swamp. "Fuck, that hurt." She caught another branch to the face. Each time, swearing they cut her, but never being able to find blood. "What the fuck am I doing here." Mom would be so upset. So would Dad and Greg and Tammy and everyone else who had been so proud of her. They were so proud that she had made it out. She conquered her demons and made something of herself. She dedicated her life to helping others.

Like a drug addict turned counselor or "scared straight" style guest speaker, Adrian began to study mental health. She started as a volunteer but worked her way into a degree program and eventually became a licensed therapist. There were struggles when her old life and frame of mind came crashing through the house she had erected around herself. But she made it through, and as she rejoined society, her friends and family rejoined her as well. The people she had cut out began to reappear, smiling and wishing her well. She was able to suppress the resentment she felt, but she never forgot how quickly they disappeared when she became too "high maintenance" for them to deal with. It was never a clean break, just subtle signs. They were always too busy to meet up; they gingerly danced around conversations about happiness. They stopped sharing their feelings or successes out of some backward fear that she would resent them for being happy. Maybe she would. Sooner or later, they would disappear, making friendship increasingly difficult to maintain until she gave up. Only when she was doing well would they mysteriously pop up, talking about how long it's been and how they should catch up.

She made new friends in college, close, dramatic friends that coalesced around each other through small parties with loud music, ice luges, and trauma-dumping. Friends became family, and she declared herself relatively normal by the end of it. The voice, that horrible voice, grew quieter when she drank. A valuable tool to have, even if she probably went a little too far with self-medication. Better than hard drugs, she figured, though she did the occasional line or three of cocaine when the situation presented itself.

After college in Maryland, she got the opportunity to practice in Boston and leaped at it. Just the chance to get away, to try new things. She found a crappy, overpriced studio apartment like everyone else; she learned her way around on the T and figured out which lines to avoid and when. She commuted into her new office as best as she could, met her new co-workers, and decorated her small office. The chair she used was worn and sterile. She had always imagined it would be a rich, thick leather or at least a cushioned cotton with floral patterns. She had no reason to assume, besides some Freud stereotypes. But what she got was neither. A low, vinyl arm chair with edges starting to crack and split. The spring cushion had exposed bits of foam beginning to peak through. 'Everyone gets the old chair when they start out,' her sponsor told her. 'When someone leaves, you'll take theirs, and the next new kid gets the old one,' he snickered with a friendly smile.

"Do people leave often?" She asked him.

"Yes, all the time. You'll see. Burn out is real, and therapists are particularly susceptible to it." He had explained. "The pay is okay, but a few months of listening to an even mix of horrifically depressing stories and whiny kids bitching about their parents will take its toll. Some are just more resilient than others. Some therapists, I mean."

"How long have you been here?" Adrian asked, trying to hide her consternation.

"Three years, but I'm not a therapist. I just work at the front desk. I see people come and go a lot. Anyway, good luck, kid." He smiled as he left her to get set up.

Sitting in the chair at work, she felt like she was doing something. Not just something, something good. And for the first few weeks, she felt happier and more useful than she ever had. The voice had gone for good; she shared the burdens with her patients and joined in their successes. But months went by, and the routine got heavier. Heavier on her soul until she felt nailed to her bed in the morning, trying to convince herself to emerge from the cave. She had felt purpose, drive, happiness. But now there was only grey. It had started warm but cooled over time. Another bout of depression, another simmering anxiety case. The stakes felt low. She supposed all therapists must feel that way sometimes. But they shouldn't feel so angry. If one more student came in to discuss midterm stress, she felt like she'd explode. She began to feel like her father. Ready to give them 'something to cry about.'

She had been betrayed. She betrayed herself. It had been going so well. The nightmares had stopped. She had escaped. The shrieking death of that horrible voice. Penetrating her soul. Wounding so deep she could never be clean. Staining her very imprint on space and time. But she had escaped. Years ago, she picked up her two suitcases, filled them with everything she could, and left the rest. She would have lit the apartment on fire if not for the families she knew lived there. And nothing could burn the stain from that horrible place.

But she had escaped. Left for the northeast. The pay was much better; she could afford a nice, albeit small, place outside the city. Begin her life again and find someone to share it with. She met Greg through a mutual friend and started a relationship. She was happy.

"Fuck!" Not today, though; today, she slid down into the muck as the ground squelched beneath her foot, subsuming her new hiking boots and sinking her up to her knee. "God, what am I doing here?"

She had been happy with Greg until Rebecca killed herself and murdered her daughter. So sudden, so tragic. Leaving her husband to wander (what was his name again?). God, what a bitch. How could someone so bright have been so evil? Is that what drove Greg and her apart? Or was it an acknowledgment of something that had existed for longer? He was so goddamn sympathetic. "You're a therapist," he would argue; "shouldn't you understand she was going through mental health issues?"

"Fuck that," she'd reply. "Pain and suffering and crazy all exist. Suicide is the ultimate expression of self-autonomy. But she killed a baby." She sobbed. "Fuck her, and I wish she could die three more times." Greg hated to argue with her, but it went on. Maybe he felt some testosterone-fueled desire to defend Rebecca. He had always liked her anyway, secretly settling for the best friend when she started dating whatshisname. Or maybe he just really cared that much?

But either way, it was tragic. And they hated each other by the end. No, that wasn't fair. Adrian hated him. Him and everyone else. She didn't think he hated her even for a moment. Not even when she showed up drunk at his house and screamed his name, just to throw a rock through the windshield of his car as he watched from the porch and called the cops.

But anyway, fuck, she was zoning again. Where was she? Still in the muck. Up to her mid-thigh at this point. Just laying her body on the wet grass. She felt the cold slither of a snake pass over her, and a faint, squelching crunch off to her right got her attention. A young wild pig walked deliberately in the same direction. Everything here, including Adrian, seemed to share a purpose. Looking around, she grabbed a stick and pulled herself. It broke. Try another. Heaving herself up, rolling off to the side and lying on her back, she looked up at the canopies of the oak trees as the sun peaked behind the hills, turning the landscape blue and grey. Night was coming, and she cried.

What the hell was she doing here? She had escaped. Until Stacey walked into her office. Talking about nightmares and anxiety and depression. An average case until she described the voice. That voice filled with the screams of animals and the demonic braying of a Hellmouth sucking in the universe. God, how it stained her. How it contorted her existence and left her unremarkable and consumed. Now she lay, not bothering to fish the tangled branches from her long black hair as the earth consumed her and hastened her transformation into some macabre death nymph from the occult horror movies of her youth.

She had escaped. She sobbed. But she came back. She had to know if she was crazy. This island was the largest in the country with a permanent population and no bridge to the mainland. Venice island. It had no value for those who didn't want to remain hidden and left alone by the outside world. Generations of inbreeding and seclusion had given the locals a soft gaze and accent that recalled northern Scotland and West Virginian hillbilly. A ferry came by once a week from the Maryland shore to drop off provisions for the grocery store. The land was too soggy for anything but crabbing. The locals had grown with an iron gut to process the increasingly polluted freshwater clams to go along with their softshell crab. It was pure. In beauty and in filth. A reminder of the natural state of the universe, carnivorous.

She knew she was crazy. She knew it. She had imagined it all for so long. But why then was this so familiar. She heard the rumbles at the airfield when the gruff, wrinkled pilot muttered to himself through his pre-flight checklist. She felt the familiar gurgling of a predator boiling within her subconscious. He circled the island and inspected the runway before landing. It recognized her.

*Go down.* Was it a command or a memory? Did she even hear it? God, what was real? She hears the whispers and screams in the background noise of the slow river, in the deafening vibration of the cicadas, in the raspy breaths of her own lungs.

*More. It's not enough. Show me more.*

That was new, different, and she felt its presence again. The horrible sounds comforted her. She wasn't crazy. Not yet. It came back. But why was it speaking to her? It spoke more clearly. It had chosen her. Why? Didn't matter. She laughed. Suddenly, feeling the elated rush of renewed purpose. She wasn't crazy. She came here for a reason. She figured it out, and she was almost there. If she had just done this before, maybe she could have stayed in Baltimore. Found love, made a living, and beat the torture of her mind. She could have had a life here.

No, she still can. Step one, get up. She sloshed over onto her stomach, enjoying the grit of the mud flowing into her shirt. Smiling into the water and heaving herself up. The ground felt solid, and she made her way to her feet, elevated by the assistance of her master. Even the voice died down. The terrified and infinite screams of a thousand animals degraded to a low rumble and static whispering in the background. It resonated with something, and she could feel the comforting relaxation spread through her core and into her brain. Her heart slowed, and her face relaxed. What was it that guy had said to her? Back when she first started talk therapy in Boston. The pineal gland? She smiled. She may have been crazy, but not that crazy.

*Not crazy at all. Come to me and submit.* Her love had taken on a new tone. Through the screaming and cacophony, she saw his true purpose. She listened through the fading terror of the animals and heard the smooth musical tones of a warm embrace. Comforting and strong. He would help her through, and she could show the world she wasn't crazy after all. She'd show him off to mom and dad and greg and rebecca and rebecca's husband and her best friend stacey back in boston and everyone else who ever cut ties or tried to get her help. They were only ever interested in getting her help when she was inconveniencing them anyway. She would show them that she wasn't crazy, that this siren song led to happiness, not death. How had she been so foolish? Why had she resisted? She would ask him when she got there. Stacey knew why she was there. She had to find the one voice that believed her, that showed she was alright. Nothing was wrong. They were all wrong.

Step two, start walking. She saw the world move around her; she stood still as the earth rotated erratically to bring her to her goal. She glanced down and saw her legs moving beneath her but had lost them. She lived only in her mind now. Relaxing in the soft cushions of a gilded cage, relishing the pampering. How nice of him to take control. She didn't have to worry anymore; she could relax. Thorns tore at her pants, but she couldn't see the blood unless she walked through the watery muck. Mahogany-brown water washed enough from her to see the pale skin below, immediately flooded by the seeping blood of her wounds that poured out until they were packed with enough debris to stem the flow.

As she traveled, she felt the air level itself. No wind, no humidity, simply perfect. The Sun stopped setting, and the dark greyish-blue sky began to brighten into a brilliant white. But why? That didn't make sense. Maybe she should check on her physical body. If for no other reason than curiosity. It didn't seem to concern her anymore. She could just relax and let herself be carried.

*You belong here. You belong to me. You belong to us.*

That sharp pit in her stomach started to grow. This wasn't right; the static began to grow in the background, beginning to grate like sandpaper against her brain; no, she wanted this; that was just her neurosis trying to ruin yet another relationship.

Silence, no static, no roaring, no comforting voice. "Just a peak," she thought as she opened her eyes; wait when did she close her eyes? The white light lifted with her heavy lids revealing the dark, clear night sky illuminated by a bright moon. Her head was craned all the way back. Looking directly upward. Her skull dangled loosely, rolling side to side along her back with each step. The rustling trees moving past told her she was still moving through the woods. Fuck, when did it get chilly? She felt pressure in her abdomen. Couldn't feel her legs, though. They felt padded with numbness like shots of Novocain.

RollingherheadtothesideShecouldn'tlifttheweightbut maybeshecouldrollitSuddenly,shewaswarmagainShewatc hedasherbodytrippedandheavedherforwardbackintothe mudHerneck,hadjerkedwithenoughforcetopitchherheadf orwardandnowshewasstaringattheground.    "This    is wrong."
ThesharpfeelinginherstomachSheknewitItwasterrorpani chorroranddespairShehadknownitsoofteninherlifeWhyw asitsofaint?AsifithadbeenhiddenbyadrugButitwasthere.

Adrian watched as her arms moved forward, burying her hands into the mud and once again lifting her body up to move forward.

"Oh my god. Oh my GOD!"
From the mud emerged what remained of her mangled legs. The left was swollen beyond recognition, clearly sprained or broken. Her knee was exposed through shredded pants, and blood oozed slowly from thick, deep gashes from the unforgiving rocks and thorns. From the right leg, the faint white tips of her tibia poked through her shin. The bone flexed as she put weight on the leg. Her fibula must still be intact because he leg held some weight, only pushing the bone out further a little at a time. Blood poured from the wounds. Christ, why couldn't she feel this? She needed to stop but watched the legs move forward perpetually, completely separated from her conscious mind and any control she once had. Her mind had always felt like it didn't belong to her, but her body had abandoned her as well. Her consciousness sat suspended. A useless accessory

attached to the only part of her existence that carried value.

*It's too late. Don't have to fight. Submit. Submit. Submit. Submit. Meat.*

The ground changed in front of her. Climbing over the roots of a large tree, she watched her right foot get caught, wedged under a gnarled and raised tree root. She was trapped. "Thank god." She thought maybe she could wait until morning or whenever this drug wore off. Maybe she would survive. Maybe she wouldn't go septic. Maybe she would wake up, and this whole fucking nightmare would be over.

"No, stop. STOP!" Her body jerked and seized. Yanking and pulling forward, completely oblivious to its peril. She heard the first real sound she had in hours. The horrible, wrenching crack of her fibula, grinding her bones into dust. Her shoe had come off in the muck already, and all that was left was the foot. Which wrenched and twisted until the jagged edges of the bones severed enough of the skin to tear from the hole. Leaving her severed shin dragging behind her as she crawled forward. Attached by only a shred of remaining flesh. As her arms reached in front of her and dragged her face along the ground, the remainder of her leg got caught on each branch and clump of grass she passed until the skin could hold no longer and tore off completely, disappearing almost completely into a puddle, leaving only the shredded flesh peaking above the surface of the water.

*Submit. Meat. Is better.*

Was she crying? Did it matter? For the love of God, let this end. I just want it to end. There is no feeling, just fear. Her body was not hers anymore. It was an object, a runaway car or train. She begged it to come back to her. But she watched the twisted forms of her arms and legs, in their wretched mutiny, drive her to oblivion.

*It's not enough. Never enough. Give us more. Where meat was been? Is more there. Give more.*

Adrian closed her eyes and thought of Greg, of Sarah the baby killer, of her brief moments of happiness in Boston. God, let this end.

*I see you. I know all. There's more there. So much more. Good meat.*

She opened her eyes one last time as her face dragged across the swamp floor. Her left eye was too filled with mud to see anymore, but through her right, she saw the looming edge of a deep pit open up ahead of her. "This is it," she knew. Please be over. She saw the world invert, and she crawled headfirst into the hole and glimpsed the pale white carapace of dozens of chittering horrors staring and cheering as she tumbled before she felt the warm black ooze that felt so familiar and plunged her into her final darkness.

# PULSE THE VOID, GET A GRIP

Stacey didn't sleep anymore. Too risky. As she stared up at the ceiling in the night, rearranging tiles in her mind and trying to keep her heart rate below a hundred twenty. She had lived her whole life with anxiety and panic attacks, but the frequency and intensity had been building for the past several months. When did it start? When John left her? When she saw that bicyclist get hit by the bus? The time blurs together when it gets this bad. Hours trudge on, forcing the sun up and down; she measures days in periods of darkness and hopes something will explode nearby to either kill her or wake her dry, mummified soul and turn her human again.

During the day and night, she wandered, looking for something worth writing about, long since having too much ambition for greatness. A few weeks of peanut butter and jelly sandwiches to just-barely pay the rent, she realized writing something good enough paid better than writing something great. Every time she wrote something that made her feel, she was punished. But the work that pays is the work that numbs and slowly splits her soul from her body. The architect of her own demise. She just separated herself from her humanity by highlighting the differences between the two. She could no longer connect, and refined her mask, the one she showed the outside world. The one that helped her survive.

"This is a newspaper, not a magazine, and certainly not your blog. Keep this shit out of your work writing. Readers aren't interested, and I especially am not." Aaron had told her. "I'm sorry to have to put it like this, but we've talked about it before. Frankly, I'm a little pissed that you tried to slip it under the radar this time." If you want to write conspiracy theories and sci-fi monster shorts, go do that, but you will not try to pass it off on this publication."

"No one else will publish it," Stacey complained, pushing her smudged, square-rimmed glasses back up to the bridge of her nose. A ritual that had its roots in the practical and psychological. She could never get them to fit quite right again after she crashed her bike on M street, swerving into a light post to avoid a car that ran a red light. Now it just became a nervous tic, and she hated it, whenever she noticed.

"Maybe because it's garbage? It's a war of the worlds knock off. You're just trying to publish vague news stories about disappearances under mysterious circumstances and imply there is something afoot, Sherlock."

"But…"

"When you put it in a newspaper, you are putting the credibility of this entire enterprise at risk in a world where journalists have so little credibility already," he continued. His softened tone trying to cushion his insults. He always tried to attenuate his meanness, saying, "I'd be nicer if I respected you less. I respect you too much to sugarcoat things."

"Aaron, I'm not making shit up!" Stacey shot back. "No one knows why people are disappearing. I'm not saying that I know for sure what it is at any point." They pulled another body from the shore near Hull. Horribly mangled, no explanation."

Aaron rubbed his face with his hands in exasperation. "I'm not arguing that at all. We've been over this. It's one thing to report the facts. It's entirely different to fill your articles with poetic language and imply the supernatural. Christ, you're writing about fucking crocodiles and chupacabras."

"I'm adding interesting comparisons to the story. Making it more interesting!" Stacey raised her voice, trying to thread the needle between passion and disrespect.

"It's more than that, and you know it. You can't add information into journalistic writing. Interesting news stories come from interesting news. You don't write stories. You find them. Keep your speculation and side-stories to another platform. I'm starting to think you actually believe this stuff. I feel like you have to because either you believe this and are starting to lose it, or you are deliberately trying to go behind my back and get yourself fired."

Stacey remained silent and fumed as her clenched fists trembled. She hated and hated beyond any reasonable anger. Aaron paused and sighed. He lifted his elbows from the desk and leaned back in his worn, vinyl chair. Looking up at the ceiling for a moment, his eyes lingered on a brown stain. Concentric blobs reaching out to show that the problem had never been completely fixed. He took a breath and slowed down his speech. "Stace, I've seen your stuff on the message boards."

Her eyebrows raised, and her stomach dropped. "What are you talking about?" She asked innocently.

"Come on Stace, let's not do this." Your article on the 11th avenue case last week was flagged for plagiarism by the software. I looked into it, and a large part of your rant was pulled from some conspiracy message board. When the team found it, they sent it to me, thinking you had stolen it. But the username is TraverseSpace97. Didn't take a genius to see that it may be Stacey Travers, who happened to have been born in nineteen ninety-seven. So, I pulled all of the posts from the board and found a pretty significant correlation between your work and these posts."

Stacey paused to weigh the cost of a lie.

"So, one of two things is happening. Either you are not posting on these sites, and you are plagiarizing, which means you are fired. Or you are writing these posts, which is not illegal but raises a lot of concerns over your ability to remain impartial and fact-oriented in your writing." Aaron stared at her, and the room filled up with silence. Stacey choked on it but stood firm. She didn't owe him anything. She locked eye contact and felt a black aura fill the corners of her vision. Suddenly, the room shrank, and she felt squeezed into an uncomfortable sea of pretense and vision and murder.

But she was still there. And Aaron broke the silence first. "Stacey, are you plagiarizing?"

"No."

"Then I need you to get your shit together if you want to continue to work here. If you need help, you'll have it. There is a space for this kind of writing. There are thousands of outlets, but this isn't one of them. If you want to get paid, you need to adhere to our standards."

"I will."

How had she become so sloppy? When she wrote, she succumbed to the deluge of thoughts and emotions that poured out of her. Trying only haphazardly to clean it up afterward. Of course, it was only a matter of time before it was a problem for her. Aaron was right, but not right in the way that he thought. He just couldn't see. He wasn't attuned to the nature of things, and he lived in blissful blindness. She looked into his eyes and saw nothing dark, nothing creeping, consuming, and shredding. She saw the pain that this assertiveness caused him, and she hated him for it.

But there was something more; only a few could see it. The blind are happiest explaining away the darkness with drug addictions, suicides and organized crime. But Stacey saw the effects of this threat, this creeping malice. All the victims were sick, all were alone, all were weakened. Some were unidentifiable, all were destroyed. The cops sometimes found just pieces with no explanation.

But all of this was useless to explain. The blind couldn't see. They couldn't hear. They couldn't hear him. He lurked in the background of Stacey's conscious mind and hid in the shadows of her darkest thoughts. It started calling in college when it reached out in vibrations and small signals in the world. A knowing glance from a stranger, a sickly dream, a flock of geese landing in unison. She called him "he" or "it" interchangeably. When the messages were stronger, they took on a personality. Violent and domineering, dangerous, but he kept calling.

When the messages got too strong, she took MDMA. Something about the euphoria quieted the drone. Helped her forget for a few days. But he always came back. And Stacey had grown to believe he was not just with her, but with others. She saw him in their eyes, along the streets, in restaurants behind smiles and lies and tears. There was a special blackness inside the skull, one that showed her who could see.

But none of this changed the fact that she needed to eat and pay rent. So, the first thing she did was delete her message board accounts.

∞ ∞ ∞

# BOSTON SCHOOL BUSSES ARE FAILING DISADVANTAGED STUDENTS: WITHOUT AN EASY WAY FOR PARENTS TO REPORT FAILURES, WE WILL NEVER SOLVE THE PROBLEM.

*By Stacey Travers, Columnist for Boston Globe*

"I'm sorry this happened; it's not like I can do anything about it, though." The Boston Public Schools (BPS) phone operator sounded calm but tired. "I'll note the problem. The bus should be there in an hour or two."

In the first ten days of school, the bus was late eight times. Bret Saunders' is new to the area and explained his frustrations to me on the curb as they waited for the bus to take his two elementary-aged children. "Not a little late, 30 to 90 minutes late. The other two days, it didn't show up at all. I spent two hours on hold with the BPS transportation department, trying to request information and file a complaint."

It got slightly better throughout the year, though his stop was skipped or canceled more than eight times. One driver got into a verbal altercation with a parent who watched on the GPS tracker as the bus idled in a parking lot for 25 minutes in Roxbury, only to arrive 35 minutes late. Back-up buses take different routes, usually missing the pickup spot and forcing parents to sprint down the sidewalks, waving their arms to flag them down.

Boston needs a simple reporting mechanism for parents. It needs to be accessible, multi-lingual, and short enough to complete in two minutes. Most importantly, the data must be made public to embrace accountability and set benchmarks. Only through simple and reliable data collection will the city be able to accurately diagnose and treat the problem.

Busing is a complex issue, and one small upset or delay can have cascading effects across the city. This is a persistent problem going back decades, and unsurprisingly, only one company submitted a bid for the contract last year. Like with many complex system failures, there are multiple causes. Decoupling school assignments from home addresses, meant to increase equity, has increased strain on an already failing bus system. Students in the same apartment complex enroll in multiple different schools, and with longer distances to travel, fewer students can walk. As a result, the number of children riding and the average length of the routes increases. Add some morning commuter traffic, and getting Saunders' kids to school has turned into a Gordian knot of "we're doing the best we can" emails. Boston will never be able to solve the problem until we understand its scope and drivers.

Right now, the only way to track a bus failure is for parents to spend 20 to 40 minutes on hold or to find and fill out a 20-field support ticket on the BPS helpdesk webpage. This is an impossible task for exasperated parents who are late for work after dropping their kids off in a rideshare.

A reporting mechanism alone will not solve these problems. At a minimum, the data collected must be made public. Public, up-to-date data on the problem demonstrates to parents and the community that the city and the school district are taking the problem seriously. This will increase participation in the reporting process and give the public visibility of the progress made. Governments and firms often hesitate to be transparent due to fear of backlash. However, public data, especially if unflattering, can be an opportunity. It forces organizations to set and achieve goals and provides a platform to showcase their improvements.

There are several high-profile examples of public data increasing accountability and sparking change. At the BBC, the 50:50 project dramatically increased women's on-screen representation just by keeping track of it. The 2001 ACT Report stressed data transparency and goal setting to increase diversity, equity, and inclusion in the tech industry. Boston needs to embrace the power of transparency to achieve public goals if we are to solve this problem.

School choice is meant to empower families to find the school that suits their child's needs. It is supposed to degrade the cycle of inequity that forces underprivileged children into poorly performing schools. But Boston's current system explicitly harms children who are new to the community and families without cars. Residents cannot send their children to better schools if they cannot rely on the school bus to get them there. The students of Boston deserve better. We can't pat ourselves on the back for improving equity when all we are doing is hiding our problems in a black box.

∞ ∞ ∞

Stacey was seventeen when Sean died. It was right around his birthday, so he was either fifteen or sixteen. Everyone assumed an overdose. That's what junkies did, they overdosed. He had disappeared before, for days and sometimes weeks. Her parents were terrified every time. But after five or six, terror turned to despair. Terror had no purpose. There was nothing they could do. The first few times he showed up at night, they found the refrigerator open and emptied. He sometimes didn't' make it to his bed; they found him asleep in the hallway, not quite snoring, just the peaceful, raspy rhythm of the dying.

She heard him whisper to himself in his room. A sorry rant about monsters and demons. He sounded like he was trapped in a never-ending onslaught of his addictions. "Go down," he would mutter. "What does that even mean?" When he heard her soft footsteps brush against the splintering wooden floors, he would shudder. "Go away," he sobbed. "There's nothing here for you."

She had done what most family members do in those situations. She tried to "snap him out of it," alternating between love and caring conversations and blind rage. They had been so close for so long. But he died long before his body, and they were no longer siblings. Her parents did the same, living in perpetual grief for a death that never happened to initiate the healing process. They left the doors unlocked so he could come home and sleep when he did. When they found their jewelry missing, along with all their food and one of the televisions, they convinced themselves it was unrelated. At least they pretended for Stacey's sake.

It's just grief, constant and unblunting grief like an infected wound that festers and festers without end but just won't kill you.

The last time he disappeared, Stacey had gotten used to it. She hadn't awoken expecting to see him, so who could really say how long he'd been gone. The mornings had taken on a normal, albeit bleaker tone. They talked less in the kitchen than they used to. Her mother hardly talked at all when she was sober. She just gave a tight hug that always threatened to turn into tears as Stacey rushed out the door to her car for school. Dad was gone in the mornings. He left earlier and came back later. Whether it was longer hours at work, avoiding coming home, or an affair, she never found out or cared to know.

School was a distraction but not a reprieve. Heroin was consuming the town like so many others. Everyone was either shooting up or grieving the slow decay of their family members, often both. Padma's father was found on the side of Route 37 two months ago. Sam Wilson's brother was shot by police officers when he pulled a gun during a raid. LaShauna Stephenson was found four months ago in the upstairs bathroom.

When drugs take a town, the evidence piles up on the sidewalks, so any visitor passing through can see the signs. The lawns get overgrown, and the smaller stone or brick buildings are boarded up with broken windows. Faded signs hang above doors with the names of the previous owners. Dick and Terry's Grocer, Renford and Sons automotive. Lasting gravestones to the death of their dreams for a better life for their children. Small heaps of trash pile up. Sometimes, blown by the wind, other times littered around a houseless camp of tents and tarps. She would occasionally peak into the camps or check the faces of addicts passed out on the sidewalks. They were never Sean. Weeks went by, and every day, she woke up wondering if he was alive. She walked into school, looking around for someone to rush up to her, saying, "I'm so sorry," and giving her a big hug.

"About what? What happened?" She would ask, already feeling her chest cave in as she would know the answer.

"Oh no, you haven't heard?" They would ask as fear and tears welled from their eyes. They wouldn't have expected to be delivering the news.

"No." Stacey would respond.

"They found Sean. Rebecca C.'s brother found him last night." Rebecca C.'s brother was a local cop. He spent most of his time finding ODs and administering NARCAN.

But that conversation never came. After two months, Stacey began to wonder if she'd ever see Sean again. The cops never found him. A hiker did. Or at least part of him. In the mouth of their dog as they walked up the mountain trails in the Blue Ridge.

There wasn't enough to confirm toxicology. It was too late. They'd never know if he died as a result of his own choices, by overdose or murder, or mountain lion attack or suicide. There was no end. He was just erased. What the fuck is closure anyway? Just permission to complete the grieving process. They had a partial answer, but Stacey knew better. They would never get their closure, and it was often too much for Mom and Dad. Eventually, they just chose what they believed in and compartmentalized it. That's what junkies did, they disappeared. But Stacey knew better. She had heard the silent struggles he faced. And when she flopped onto her bed one evening after years of exhaustion and anxiety, she heard the dark whisper begin to echo through the walls, and she knew Sean was something more. *Go downnn.*

# BODY FOUND ON THE RIVERBANK

*By Stacey Travers, lead contributor, Boston Globe, Sep 20.*

Police removed a mutilated body from the bank of the Charles River near MIT, east of Massachusetts Avenue, this morning at approximately five o'clock. Police have not yet released the identity of the person as they attempt to locate next of kin, but locals in the neighborhood of lower Cambridge have speculated on the identity. Three individuals have unofficially identified the body as a 56-year-old homeless man known as "Twelve percent." Residents of the neighborhood and two homeless residents confirmed that the man, normally a common sight on morning commutes, hadn't been seen for several weeks.

The body was discovered by Mr. Patrick MacArthur, a local resident walking down to the banks of the river along his familiar route to his favorite fishing spot near the Mass Ave bridge.

MacArthur (62) walked his familiar route to the riverbank just as he has for the last twenty-five years on September 3rd when he noticed dark stains on the rocks. Upon investigating, MacArthur discovered the body washed up on the rocky shore, partially eaten by birds and bloated from what police assume was a significant amount of time in the water. The man appears to have been mauled by some animal, as he had multiple lacerations on his face, torso, and limbs. His right arm and both of his legs had been severed and have yet to be recovered by search crews. Police declined to comment until after the investigation but were overheard mentioning that only one body had been discovered so far. Police boats spent the rest of the day searching along the banks for the remainder of the corpse.

MacArthur declined to be interviewed by the media but told investigators that it wasn't the first body he had found.

In the 1980s, during the peak of organized crime in Boston, the Charles River was a familiar disposal area for murder victims due to the opacity of the brackish and polluted water. As many as 16 murder victims were pulled from the water between 1987 and 1989 during a particularly violent confrontation between Whitey Bolger's crime family and elements of the

Italian mafia operating out of the North End. During that time, MacArthur appeared twice in police reports after finding two separate victims on two unrelated occasions. He was even briefly considered a person of interest according to documents obtained through a Freedom of Information Act request. But police found no indication that MacArthur was in any way connected to the murders and chalked it up to the local currents carrying bodies that familiar bend in the river after being disposed of from as far west as Watertown.

Despite this history, police seem unconcerned that this is an indicator of a return to organized crime in the Boston metropolitan area. One officer, commenting under the condition of anonymity after the body was removed, stated that the man was likely mauled by a large animal or pack of animals. Lacerations were inconsistent with torture or sharp weapons; his arm had been torn off and possibly consumed, as they have yet to find the remaining pieces. He had also been crudely cut in half at the torso, and the victim doesn't match the profile of an organized crime victim or perpetrator. He was unwilling to speculate on what kind of animal could have conducted such a violent and vicious attack. American black bears are rarely seen venturing through the miles of suburbs into the city and rarely attack humans. Mountain lions are all but extinct in the region, with only two encounters on record with enough evidence to confirm, one in 1997 and another in 2011, according to Mass.gov. However, even without meeting those rigorous standards, the last reported Mountain Lion attack in Massachusetts was in 2003, 80 miles west in the town of Sunderland. Residents are encouraged to take precautions when traveling at night until the cause of death is determined.

Locals described the victim as kind but tormented. He was most commonly spotted along Avenue J, walking in circles and muttering to himself. Sarah Berkens (36) encountered him regularly on her walk to the bus stop en route to her nursing job at Mass General. She described him as kind and outgoing on most days, saying, "he had a good soul, but when you saw him, and he rocked his head back and forth, shaking his arms and slapping himself in the face, you knew that you should walk on the other side of the road." She said he never hurt anybody that she was aware of, but he wasn't himself all the time. Twelve percent appeared to suffer from a mental condition that precluded him from engaging in society.

As police await a full autopsy report and attempt to contact any living relatives, the rest of us are left to ponder. What could have done this? If you or someone you know has any information that may be related to this case, Police have asked that you report it ASAP.

∞ ∞ ∞

# THE NEW BLACK DHALIA:
# SOMETHING IS KILLING THE LOCALS

*Posted on September 21, by @TraverseSpace97*

I got a peak at the corpse yesterday. If you didn't hear, it was reported in the Globe. Man finds mutilated body washed up along the riverbank near Mass Ave. It only gave a few details, but I saw the body, and it was worse than you could imagine.

I was running the loop along memorial drive and across the Mass Ave bridge to the esplanade. Summer's second wave has faded, and the air is beginning to crisp. The morning air stayed warm enough to coax you outside in a t-shirt, but the eastern wind coming off the ocean made you regret it. The morning was grey, like so many others. It slowly saps the dopamine from your synapses, little by little, preparing you for the dark winter ahead.

The first thing I noticed was the smell. The salt air and decaying fish and seaweed smell that is usually reserved for the harbor. But there was no salt in it, and the acrid whisp of roadkill that briefly filled my nostrils. I looked down toward the water and saw a man on his phone on the brass near a clump of reeds leading to the school boathouses.

I passed my usual turn on to the bridge and followed the path toward the man and the smell. He was a small, gruff, and balding man in his sixties. Perhaps, to someone, he was a caring grandfather who was just never the same after gram died. Perhaps he was the father who alienated his family with racist remarks on thanksgiving.

An older man, a faded ball cap, dressed in layers like any good New Englander. His long white beard nearly covered the gold chains around his neck. One cross, one star of David, and one crescent. He caught eyes with me as I approached and slowed down. "Yeah, it's a body, I think, near MIT." He rasped into the phone with a voice that sounded like cigarette smoke and bourbon. In his eyes, I saw fear, and caring, and disgust. When he met my gaze, he shook his head briefly, signaling that I should stay away. But I've never been one for rules, I suppose. I turned my gaze to the disturbed bed of reed that the man must have emerged from. Through the grey outline dawn afforded, I could see a dark mass. I stumbled off of the sidewalk onto the grass, walking toward the reeds without acknowledging the man's protest.

What fresh hell awaits us all? The writhing lump of meat that was once a person, presumably with a soul. How must God feel about the way his creation was treated? I suppose if he wasn't the one who mutilated him so unceremoniously. I imagine it's akin to a toddler cutting the hair off its dolls. Happy to do it themselves, but jealous and possessive when others want to do the same.

The thing, and thing it was, no longer human, was heaped onto the shore. It was not splayed out, spread-eagled in the muck, but rolled into a ball, at first glance, looking like it might be standing up, just a normal person trapped in the mud. Hunching to one side and propping up his body with one arm.

But then, where is the other arm?

And your mind begins to make sense of the sight as if the dawn broke faster and carefully painted the scene before your eyes. Those light-colored glints, cracked and gnawed bones emerging from the chest. The round edge of the shoulder is of a torso lying on its side. The organs, mostly gone, leaving the remaining flaps of skin and muscled to drape over the remaining ribcage like a couch cover. Yes, I could see the ragged edges dangling in the shallow water and the glistening movement of the liquid river muck flowing in and out of an empty chest cavity.

Walking around to the far side, the head was angled unnaturally, allowing the crown of the head to dip into the river while the face stayed above. It looked like one eye remained, the other unceremoniously removed, leaving what remained of the optic nerve dangling toward the mouth. The lips hung swollen and limp, revealing the teeth and holes in the gums that exposed the skull beneath. As I walked closer, two furry rats scurried out of the way, the first emerging from the chest and the second squeezing its way through a hole in the neck, punctured by the sharp end of a right clavicle.

So familiar. The numb shock that engulfed me. That combination of terror and boredom. It shot me back in time to the day they found Sean's hand in the swamp. It was all they ever found. Now, on the banks, that miasma resurfaced and clawed at my throat, choking me. When I stole a glimpse of his hand through the swinging door of the morgue, it branded the image in my mind. MY mom silhouetted against the fluorescent lights as she collapsed to the floor. I saw the glint of his middle finger tattoo and the ring he stole from dad the last time he was home. The image faded eventually, resurfacing only when I drank alone or had a sudden jump scare. It's a heavy, energetic numbness that leaves you physically tired every time.

In the banks, I burned the images in my mind and shuffled quietly back to the man on the phone, who was no longer on the phone but staring at me cautiously without call or signal. We stood a few feet apart, neither wanting to acknowledge the beauty and peace of the morning as the sun clawed its way above the city skyline and began to wash the scene in pink and orange. The steady rush of cars increased as commuters went happily on their way, oblivious to the darker display of the natural world.

He allowed a tear to escape his furrowed face and stretched his throat, desperately trying to regain control. "Animal attack, I guess." He quivered out in a peaking mix of fear and sorrow. I nodded but didn't look away. There it was, in his eyes. He knew, as I did, that this was different. He, like I, envied the corpse. We felt it's release. The end of its suffering. I felt the pressure in my body as the soul pushed and heaved and cracked its way out.

∞ ∞ ∞

# THE TYRANNY OF FALSE DICHOTOMY
*Posted on October 13, by @TraverseSpace97*

Diametric learning strategies are critical to breaking schema and building critical thinking skills, but we run the risk of falling into the same trap. Boiling the complex reality of existence into a series of falsely opposite, oversimplified schema instead of one.

We must accept that dichotomies are useful tools, but still very much on the order-side of the organizational spectrum. Chaos, order, and everything in between must be considered. Because people will simultaneously have infinitely diverse perspectives, and bin themselves (and others) into simplified, organized groups.

While credentials lend utility and uniformity of language to an argument, we cannot exclude "genius," even if some turn out to be crackpots. The term "genius" itself is simply an overly reverent label for divergent thinking.

What strategic thinking needs as a discipline is a sober acknowledgment that ordered thinking and divergent thinking must be equal partners in the discussion, not just that ordered systems are broken. Strategy is not the search for solutions; it is adept navigation through stormy waters. Strategy is neither an organized, accessible process nor a chaotic clairvoyance of divergent thinkers. It both. The purpose and core of strategic thinking is in the balanced friction between order and chaos, analysis and imagination, history and forecasting.

The levels of understanding:

1) Lack of understanding

2) Understanding through one schema

3) Meta understanding of 1-n schema. This is where critical thinking resides.

4) Meta- meta-understanding of the fabricated nature of the concept of schema.

Bounded rationality – losing a sense of the framework of reality can lead to nihilism and depression. Centering methodologies such as monotheistic religion relieve the mind of the need to comprehend. Serves as a friendly conversation ended, as it were. Recognizing the fallacy of one's own schema is breaking away from the first level of the human mind. But most stop there and sit comfortably above the rest. But they fall into the very same trap at the higher cognitive level. They force complex ideas into false dichotomies and choose between them.

The next level is the synthesis model. Taking the thesis and antithesis and setting them against each other to create a synthesis. This is where most "smart" people lay. They get truth and credibility by quoting other, socially acceptable smart people. Their intelligence is limited to recall and rapid understating of concepts.

But at what point does the brain begin to generate new information? Or is that asymptotic in nature? Can the mind get closer but never achieve truly novel ideas. Our very ability to think is bounded by language. Moreover, our non-lingual ability to think is shaped by our environment. Did we get enough food as children? We're we safe? Interested? Supported? Did we have sunlight?

∞ ∞ ∞

## HAVE YOU EVER TRIED TO RELAX?
*Posted on November 2, @TraverseSpace97*

When you die, there is no shortage of people to declare your sainthood. Use the last of the good scotch to bring the last good sleep. It's as though they drag on the epic of your life only to assure themselves that their actions, their essence will remain imprinted on the collective consciousness. I am not worthless; I am not worthless. I matter. My life matters. This desire is almost universal. In religions, the surviving convince themselves and others that the dead are good people as if arguing the case to their god as the dead lay in wait at the gate. Seeing nothing, seeing everything. In an infinite reality, emotions and moments are meaningless. Not in the popular sense, meaning poor or low meaning, literally without meaning or undefined. But when reality is infinite, those feelings and moments have the same value as enlightenment and lifetimes. Those lifetimes have the same value as all of existence. Without meaning. When the sun goes down, will you step up? Will I? Is this what I meant all of this time. Some burdens in life cannot be lifted; they can only be carried. They say it's unhealthy to hold it all. But when you cannot burden, only damage, it is better to localize the damage. What a great paradox that talking about your emotions is so popular that the very act of expressing pain devalues it. Suffering is not suffering unless it is silent.

When they declare everyone is the best of us, who is the best? If I dedicate my life to safeguarding and carrying anything I can, for everyone I can. If I sacrifice myself entirely, am I the best of us? If so, how will we know when the same person can die after decades of being a nice gas station attendant and is declared equally ideal. When convicted rapists live the rest of their lives harmlessly, and their loved ones claim sainthood. Self-sacrifice. Beyond tradition and definition. True sacrifice is knowing, not believing, you will not be remembered. The stories will fade in a generation, pictures will be lost, there will be no annals of your adventures. Your loved ones will remember you, but they will die also. There is no greater reward, and your sense of honor is a fiction. But sacrificing, nonetheless. I don't even like scotch.

Am I the best or the worst? How much different would my life have to be? What would tip the scales and turn me into a serial killer? Would it take only one? What got me here when there were so many opportunities to go the other way. Please excuse the man in the corner; he doesn't seem to notice that his chest caved in. I don't feel better. Now, I guess the aim is not to feel. The worst part is not knowing. Brought into a tumultuous time. The sky is the limit, but so are the depths. Brought into a world of false sorrow. How do you raise a child with real problems in a world of fake ones?

Don't think about it.

Don't think about it.

You can stare at the corners all night long; all you'll do is see them move.

Imposing figures in your mind, sharpened, taught, and grim.

Your chest collapses and disappears, drowning in your breath.

Breathing halted, limbs are numb, frozen withered, slim.

Don't think about it.

Don't think about it.

From our perspective, time is constant. Imposing, willful, wrath.

Nothing changes, nothing helps, and nothing ebbs the flow.

The pain you feel is life itself; there will be no respite.

You try to find catharsis, but the suffering is too slow.

Don't think about it.

Don't think about it.

So they try to talk you down again. "If there's anything I can do."

Their near-attempt solution confines you to your fate.

Keeping busy, taking stock, be patient yet again.

To appear as if there's hope and you are not resigned to hate.

Don't think about it.

Don't think about it.

# BECCA'S NOTE

Turning through a winding road.
Hair anticipates the wind.
Pores contract to shield the chill.
Skin stretching tight, fleeing the coming
challenge.
Inevitable. It's dark before the end.
There is no honor in the plunge,
not without choice.
But to let it in, to submit to the change.
Chest collapsed, leaves us shrinking
evermore.
We stop clawing,
and submit.

-- *"All Roads Converging" by H.M. Sackler*

I've never liked writing, I almost didn't bother with this, but you deserve something of an explanation. You've earned that much. I know you'll never forgive me, but just maybe this will help you understand. Sometimes, good people must sacrifice their goodness, must do horrible things to help good flourish and prevent evil from thriving. I was driven to this point. Whatever you choose to believe, please don't ever think that I wanted this to happen, or that I wouldn't have taken every possible measure to do something else if there was any hope at all.

When we met, I think I knew this was all going to happen. I knew there was a darkness in me, and I knew that yours and mine would not cancel out, but drive each other down, but I wouldn't stop it. You made the same sly jokes and charming smiles, and I faltered. "Just one more day." This was always coming for me. And one more day with you was a day with the darkness at the fringe. But it was never going to last. Then you proposed, and on the night before the wedding, I cried and cried, wondering why I would let myself do this. I saw the end coming. But one more day with you and the darkness was on the fringe. It crept closer, like a blood disease, penetrating silently into my body. I knew it was waiting for me, but one more day with you and it couldn't take me.

The night of our wedding, I made the final error. I hoped. I felt love, light, and happiness. For that moment, I lay beside you, watching you sleep, and forgot that I was doomed. I saw a future of love and happiness, and I put the darkness out of sight. But when it hides, it grows and prepares. So, we played the game like gamblers, hopelessly postponing the inevitable fall. Betting and betting, chasing losses with each failure, increasing the perceived likelihood of the next remarkable success.

When we found out about her. I felt it stir again, but I ignored it, and it grew. I buried my doubts in vitamins and nesting and food. I excused the familiar feelings, blaming pregnancy brain and hormonal changes. I was desperate to make it work. Then she was born, and when she came, I felt it again, stronger than ever. It reached out through me, and I tried to fight it, but it passed through me and into her. When I saw her eyes, I died. Nothing could match the horror. I saw it in her eyes. The darkness stared back at me. She was infected. I had doomed her.

You have it, too. You know it. You feel it when you stop to think. It hides in the corners of your brain even now. Just pause; don't look away from this page. Now breathe twice, slowly. Feel all the layers of your own emotion recede. Feel the goosebumps rise along your neck and back. It lies beneath. That heavy silence that pulls you down just so slightly. The weight in your throat feels like crying, even when you think you are happy. Now, feel him. He lies just beyond the periphery of your sight. Don't look away from this page. There is a special pressure in the bottom of your throat. How does it feel like it's closing and stretching at the same time? I always imagine being choked, but I still breathe. Like the inside is closing, but the neck is expanding.

Don't look away from this note. Stay focused here. He's right beyond your perception now. He's there; can't you feel him? He's always just outside of reach. That flickering light? That shifting curtain, the shadow never cast. But in your room, the lights are gone, and the curtains are still. There is no draft. It's him. He's circling, waiting to strike. A hulking, rapacious mass of flesh and toxin slithering its way behind you. Ready to sink its fangs into the back of your neck.

Do you feel him now? As he wheezes that horrible wheeze. Tickling the back of your neck as it waits to grab hold. He never leaves; he just hides in the dark places, waiting. He never even grants the finality of death. Just waiting, just lusting, just breathing in the chasms along the edges of perception. I don't want that for her. I hope you find us before we decay. I know this can be messy.

I don't sleep anymore. I lie with my eyes closed next to you and try not to kill us both. It's been that way for months. You lie awake like me for hours until you finally pass out, usually around one. Then I wander, grab the gun, and hold it to your head. I hold it to my own. I hold it to hers. But I have always been too scared to follow through. And I stash it back in the case above your suits. It's your decision to make, not mine. I hope you choose something better, but the baby, she still has a chance. So, I had to be sure. I wanted to be absolutely sure I wasn't crazy.

So, I tested. I watched her. I stared into her eyes and soul every day. I withered away, feeding her and staring into the darkness. It never receded, not once. I watched her laugh, and the darkness stayed. I watched her cry, and it grew. I saw the emotion blur into blackness every day like it was all a façade covering the human truth. I have no doubts now. It has her, and it's my fault. It reached her through my worthless body. I tried to save her without resorting to this. I had her baptized while you were away. I know it's usually a bigger ceremony, but I told Father Reagan that it was urgent, so he let me stop by the church and did what he could. I knew you wouldn't approve, but it wasn't for you. She had to be clean. I'm already going to rot and sting and burn in hell. She can be saved. And that is all that mattered.

For a moment, I thought the darkness receded in the quiet emptiness of St. John's, but it was only a trick of the light gleaming through the stained-glass walls. I didn't recognize the scene; you know I was a bad catholic growing up. One of the ones with Mary. For a moment, I allowed myself the briefest hope. But seeing the light fade away as quickly as it had come. It follows. It followed. Just as it follows you now as you read this. And so, I have no more options.

I never wanted it to be this way. I know you think you understand, but you don't. You can't, even when you try. I thought I was safe. I thought I had escaped. I did escape. But it didn't last. So, I had to. My mother had it, I have it, and he's trying to take our daughter. I couldn't let that happen. This is better. The horrific sight of her mangled corpse still burns my mind, and it's been thirty years. There is no end to the suffering but death. Hell awaits me, but not her. I will save her while she's innocent. I hope to see you again someday. But I know I won't. You won't forgive me, and I know you shouldn't. But I WON'T LET HIM HAVE HER. Not like he's had me. I hope you find us before we decay. I know this can be messy.

Even as I write this, I hear him. He is getting stronger, and he has reached into my soul, staining me. Burning me. When I resist, he punishes me. I can only submit. This will not get better. I won't end up like Mom. I won't. And I'll save the baby (I can't bring myself to write her name). But please know that. I'm going to save her. This is better. I hope you save yourself, too.

It's done, I'm shattered. She's at peace. She didn't even struggle; I made sure the water was warm. Hopefully, she remembered the womb. The last bit of peace and comfort she had, even if it was inside me. And here I am, ready to follow. Well, not follow; I'm taking a different path. I hate myself and you and everyone but her. But I know she's better now. She's safe from the fate that you and I share. Now, I'm starting at the bathtub as it continues to fill. I got the toaster and the extension cord. But still, I hesitate. There is no going back now. I wonder if she would have forgiven me if she ever got the chance. I hope you find us before our bodies decompose too much. I know this will be messy. I turned the faucet down, but it'll probably spill all over everywhere when I thrash. Electrocution is violent if the movies tell any truth at all. And if that doesn't work, if the toaster has an emergency fuse or something, I've got the pistol ready. I'm resolved. This isn't a cry for help. It's just a courtesy, so you don't have to spend the rest of your life wondering what happened.

Why can't I stop thinking about shooting myself? No matter how hard I try during all of this. Even when he is silent, I get a moment alone and fantasize. It hardly matters now. But did you honestly never feel it? I always assumed you were just trying to be supportive. You must have felt it, right? The pressure in your skull that can't escape. It builds behind nose and eyes and tear ducts; it builds and begs to be set free. It's such a comforting thought, the cold, sharp pang of the steel barrel on the fleshy part under my jaw. That thick meat that seems ripe for piercing. Do you never just fantasize about sharpening a coat hanger or picture wire and running it through your jaw, pushing up through your tongue, and wiring into your cheeks and eyes? Feeling the scrub of frayed wires as they eviscerate your temples and the back of your sockets? It can't be just me. I know you've been to the dark places as well. I know you've seen through the veil of this bullshit reality. ~~Frankly, maybe everything would be better if you would stop fucking pretending that everything is alright all the time. This is fucking real, and you know it. If anything, you could have stopped all of this to begin with if you had just paid the fuck attention and listened to me. But I always fucking knew you couldn't. You were always a weak piece of shit. God, how many times did I just try to talk to you? But you would never listen. Not once, you fucking fuck. God I hate you so much and I'm angry all of the time and there is nothing that would have ever prevented this because you're such a weak fucking man. There were so many signs! So many but you pretend and pretend and pretend because you're a tiny weak worthless bitch! Fuck you! Fuck you! FUCK YOU.~~

I'm sorry. I don't mean any of that. I could have started over with a new sheet of paper, but that hardly seems to be important at this point. You did the best you could. But neither of us can keep him at bay. He is all-knowing and all-consuming. There is no escape for us. But there was for her. I saved her the pain of this life. She will move on to the better things. If only all our parents had the decency to make this sacrifice, our whole fucking species would have been saved. The dissonance is too powerful. It's such a burden, so I'll end here.

I really did love you, as best as I could. But I wasn't strong enough to defeat him. He's coming for us all.


There are colors too bright for light to retain.
There is darkness too violent for the soul to restrain.
And when he comes knocking with blood on his
   hands,
the rest all come flocking to call you insane.


Wretched your brain and ravished your plans,
the quiet one shudders while the dead one stands.
He'll suckle your corpse. On death, he reigns.
They'll come for you, as if murderous clans.


In the name of your freedom, they bind you in chains
until broken and ravaged, your corpse, it remains.
When he crushes the door, to harvest your soul,
they will rush to the floor, to spit-shine the stains.


Now beaten your corpse, blackened as coal.
To submit to the pain, consuming you whole.
He suckles away the marrow and bone.
And you'll never regain your chance at a soul.


And the rest? They receded, cursing your name.
Your colors, they blinded. Their eyes, white, remain.
Their marrow, their bones, safe from his grasp
But among them, the tortured start gliding to pain.

Do the right thing. I hope I'm lonely in hell. It would
   mean you escaped.
-- B

# CONSUME ALL

The pale, exoskeletal, crustacean shell glowed faintly in the darkness. Thick fog in the air and mind, hollowing out perception in both sight and thought. The creature, formless in its intent, cold, impersonal. Not angry or cruel, but suddenly ruthless, robotic, exacting, and unstoppable. A long claw for cutting, a short one for gripping. It had one purpose, to collect. Lurching over the heap of prey that collected in the pit. Sometimes, prey came in faster than it was processed, and quivering bodies suffocated in filth under the weight of those that followed.

The ooze that slopped onto the pit softened the flesh and paralyzed the nerves but did not poison. Food watched itself decay and waited for collection, like maggots eating their way out of the still-living body of their host. Food just watched. Sometimes, the bigger ones lurched out of the pit. But they were easier to collect. The terrors did not have to search for their connections within the tangled heap. They scuttled over and collected the meat, an ever-growing mound of flesh and rot.

Today, she lurched over the matted fur of the quivering animal and felt it husk out a breath of whimpering fear. She reached for the limp, soggy meat. The dog didn't move but let out a soft, breathy whine as it came into the grip of the hanging terror perched from a catwalk. She stretched her claw down to the heap below and found the poor animal's paw. She pulled slowly from the muck. A weak bark and exasperated shiver, in a last burst of sad defiance, the poor thing loosed itself from death's grip. It slipped the claw and tried to run, managing only a seizure of spastic muscle twitches as its bloodshot and terrified eyes searched desperately for help. Its whole body shivered in the muck, gasping and whinnying.

He briefly escaped the horrific grasp of lurking claws. But victory was fleeting and sullen. The sharp arm emerged from the catwalk. A muffled crack of bones as the long claw pierced slowly through the chest, shattering the ribs and eviscerating his lungs. A whimper, a gurgle, and the panicked heaving as its lungs filled with fluids and collapsed. The terror pinned its prey as it pried the hind leg. If it knew the animal was alive, it showed no sign.

No more air to shriek, the horrible gurgling of the dog as its hip dislocated. With the sharp claw in its prey, the terror pulled and pulled. The animal could no longer gurgle; its body shook and splorched in the muck. Vomit and bile spewed forth from its mouth and nostrils, mixed black with the slow miasma that consumed it. Death awaited from below; death approached from above. His eyes bulged from their sockets as he lay trapped in an eternal misery.

Christ, let it die. Please, for the love of God, let it die.

The awful, quiet tearing of skin. The leg came loose, and whatever blood and viscera remained oozed from the poor animal's lungs. Blood sprayed and poured over the terror and showered the pale shell of the creature. Hiding its glowing carapace in a dark ooze to match the floor.

∞ ∞ ∞

Despair. Old experiments, conducted before anyone cared about subject rights, showed that animals experience despair when they submit to the idea that there is no hope of escape from a painful or frightening circumstance. A dog that has access to two cages will panic and leap from one to the other if shocked, almost indefinitely. Another dog, with only one cage, will panic after the first several shocks but eventually lie down and submit. It doesn't experience the same adrenaline response. It accepts its fate. The same response is seen in mice and rats that are placed in containers of water with no escape. They thrash and thrive and panic until they are exhausted, but eventually, stop trying and wait to die.

Humans are a little different; an idea or a feeling can affect willingness to fight or carry on. While some people reach despair and shock and become helpless at the slightest provocation, others willingly seek glorious death in battle before their time. In fact, the idea of glory will drive some to fight wars with enemies they don't understand on behalf of politicians they've never met for a vague set of ideals they can't define. But glorious death has its own allure. At least until we are confronted by it. We all shit our pants in the end. Oddly enough, faith serves a perfect, dual purpose; it can inspire us to confront death only through the promise that death isn't death. That is, death isn't final. In fact, it's the beginning of something infinite. Along an infinite timeline, death has no power, no meaning. And for those in the deep, dark sight, life carries the same weight.

What presence reaches out to us in the night? That voice that whispers from the fringe, coaxing our thoughts to the dark and despair. What if we share the same voice? A lustful desire for pain and suffering and torment that exists but rises to the surface only in knowing glances exchanged between the travelers who have peered into its depths. Even among the articulate depressed, the most learned suicidals talk in codes and euphemisms to each other. Referencing "dark times" they spent in "dark places" when alluding to a suicide attempt or ideation. Social existence is a buoy on the surface of that despair. We ride the undersea currents but can only share our discoveries at the surface. Is it so surprising then, for the depraved few to imagine sharing that pain? Like an infection, they want to pass the disease onto others through violence. "Now you see," they'll exclaim at the horrified eyes of their victims. "You see the world as I do."

Furious envy. Jealousy of a life that is lost forever. The sighted beg for the comfort of the naïve. The bitter try to steal that light. Traumatized people traumatize people.

∞ ∞ ∞

Despair. As the poor dog's adrenaline subsides and its blood pressure drops, it begins to rest. The calmness of the moment belies the wrenching, electrocuting pain that engulfs its physical body and consumes its mind. But the terror subsides as it no longer has a purpose. Fear increases adrenaline, which aids survival, but when survival is off the table, submission is the only option for the body. Do the spasms of the body infect the mind, rendering him unable to string together a coherent thought?

What does he think of at that moment? Are his thoughts taken over by memories of loved ones? By playful days outside or curling up on a couch with loving owners? Does it have offspring? Does it linger on its children? Or does it linger only on pain as any remaining thoughts fade into nothingness?

∞ ∞ ∞

The whispers are not in English, or in any language. They reach out through suggestion. Think of a pistol right now. The cold steel of the barrel under your chin. The bullet spiraling in through your flesh and tongue, forcing its way into your temporal lobe and liquifying the tissues on its way through to the other side of the skull. It punctures a hole through the top and releases the existential pressure that builds and builds. Overpressure from the barrel follows and escapes behind the bullet into the new hole. It cracks the bones and turns what's left of brain into mush that jettisons outward through the exit point and scatters itself in Pollock fashion onto the walls behind you and the ceiling above. Did you feel the pressure release? Did it seem anything less than horrific? Was there a part of you, no matter how small, that didn't recoil in disgust and fear? He is inside you.

When you huddle in the corner. Hugging your knees to your chest, covering your ears with your arms, trying to keep your skull from breaking, do you suddenly think of the noose? Is there comfort in the thought? Blood trapped in your brain causing surges of endorphins and adrenaline before your heart shudders to a halt. You know it's not so peaceful, but there is comfort in the thought. It's like thinking of mulled wine on a snowy evening or the quiet release of removing your work boots at the end of a long day. He is reaching. He is searching, and he is finding, not you, not yet, but he finds.

Like most phenomena, the dedicated attention and research into suicide results in a series of splits ad infinitum. Eventually, this leads to the same conclusion as all natural things: it's a spectrum. Where once, it was a question of honor or madness, suicide became a binary construct as it was pressed into psychological study. Crazy and sad were the same thing. To be so sad that you are suicidal is analogous to insanity, especially considering the consequences pushed in Catholicism. When death was common, was there suicide? Or were the suicidal just more reckless? Berserkers in the north, sprinting naked into battle to exact terror onto the residents of well-defended villages. If that weren't an option, would they have killed themselves? Would the suicidal have been more likely to go on treacherous journeys and adventures, dying alone in the wilderness or in glorious battle? When war was less common, and civilization beat back the threats of nature, when mankind became the apex predator, and an early death was hard to find, is that when suicide became a disease? Is that when suicide became a sin?

Eventually, some classify it as a mental state or disorder. Then, the levels of suicidal tendencies begin to split. We learn warning signs and attempt to rationalize it. We differentiate between suicide attempts and suicidal ideations. Suicidal ideations begin to receive their own levels of support. Eventually, we see that as people self-identify, there are levels of suicidal ideations, and the weaker ones are further classified under such terms as "intrusive thoughts" or "morbid thoughts." Perhaps it's more normal to think about killing oneself than previously thought. Perhaps it's not necessary to force everyone who has ever daydreamt of jumping off a building into rigorous, and public, treatment programs.

Perhaps still, every human, maybe even every being, has thought about it at least once. Perhaps that is why we are so susceptible. This, of course, is a triple-edged sword, like a reinforcing loop that must be balanced. Accepting that morbid thoughts are normal may reduce one's reaction to them, but it may also normalize them. If the patient is no longer afraid of their morbid thoughts, they can grow beyond suicidal ideations. If the patient no longer differentiates between the two, they can continue to grow. What is a plan anyway? If the patient knows they would never, but still thinks of how they would kill themselves if they ever wanted to, making a plan? Like a heart attack, a sudden, dramatic episode alarms the victim and causes them to seek treatment. But a slow build-up, small panic attacks, that grow over time. High blood pressure and frightening episodes numb the victim until it's too late.

To maintain that fear of morbid thoughts, the patient may get overwhelmed and may have a stronger reaction to lighter stimuli. Would that make it just as bad or worse? The answer as always, is: it depends. The simplest definition of chaos is a group of equations with more variables than equations. You need exactly one equation for every variable in order to solve them all. Every person is the product of an infinite number of variables from genetic disposition to life experiences, to the weather of the moment to the comfort of their shoes. You can never solve all of the variables, so you will never know what the outcomes are.

Life is sailing a ship in stormy waters. The captain cannot pretend to control the environment; they can only navigate through it. Guiding their course within the situation they are given. Their route is never direct, and their success is not guaranteed, but decisions made within the system maximize their chances. Still, like in life, a captain cannot guide a ship alone. It takes networks and systems of others with shared purpose and differing expertise to stay on course. So, perhaps the greatest advice is to build the network of people that help guide you. An encouraging thought for those who can benefit from human connection. Unfortunately, not everyone can.

∞ ∞ ∞

Sean used to caw like a crow. It was our secret code to let each other know where to find the other. He was better at it than me. I stumbled in the mud trying to find him, never once sounding like a bird of any kind. In retrospect, I don't think I ever saw a crow in our backyard. He used to explain to me how they were as smart as five-year-olds and could learn to talk. I didn't believe it until I saw the videos online. He lost his way. He turned away from me, from us, from his family, and his whole life. And no amount of cawing could bring him back. Not when I led with love and tried to help. Not when I got angry and shouted. He just couldn't find his way back to us. He was always better at cawing than me. I stumbled through mud and dead leaves to find him perched in a tree overlooking the terrain. I had never wanted a tattoo, but it seemed right after the wake. There was no body to bury. Sean was lost forever. But maybe he could guide me just a little bit. He pointed me in the right direction. Or so I hoped. Ravens are as smart as five-year-olds, and they can be devious as well.

But I guess I also liked the connotation as well. Sure, crows were cliché, the terrifying birds of legend and film, symbolizing death almost exclusively, but that was the benefit. People would see the tattoo and ask about it, and she could just say she was a fan of Poe, or Kubrick, or just a fan of the bird itself. I don't have to tell them about Sean if I don't want to. I usually don't want to.

# HARVESTER

*They must have all spawned from the same pit. After all, they aren't particularly different from ants.*

In the beginning, she was smaller. But even the larvae today are bigger than their fully-grown ancestors. They crept quietly beneath the legs of the hunters, desperately picking over the scraps left behind. She frittered in the dark, endlessly following the dark's glow of warmth and aromatics that tickled her small brain. Biting away at the soft bits when she found them, scuttling away to avoid the wrath of the big ones. When successful, she ate quickly and quietly, returning to the never-ending search.

She was second, third, fourth, or last in line. For she was small, and overstepping was punished with angry nips and slashes. Endlessly searching, trying to find the kill and escape before the rest arrived. Dormancy, not sleep, rested her thin body and punctuated a tedious life. Can it be called tedious, though? Does the fish get tired of swimming? Does the hyena get tired of scavenging? There was no existence outside of the search; like a terrible ant, she executed her functions.

Sometimes, the hunters brought back too little or ate the bones and all of the small, furry things they returned. And the hunger set in. Again, if it can be called hunger. To a simpler form of life, what is the difference between feeling peckish and existential fear of death? They must be the same, for they have the same consequences. Perhaps animals' diverse range of emotions is differentiated by our perceived sense of closeness to death. When consequences are binary, life or death, only two emotions are necessary. But a broad spectrum of consequences that included social exclusion, financial debt, divorce from a loved partner, requires a broader spectrum of emotional responses.

Regardless, scarcity meant hunger, and the weak were culled. She scuttled in a fury, not the smallest, but a target. Enduring the nips and slashes of her peers until she pounced on another, driving her long, sharp spike into his brain and providing the feast to distract the others. She was ruthless, they all were, and soon learned to kill the others before the hunger set in. More prey meant she was protected from the nips and slashes and screeching calls for blood and meat. And time passed. She was successful, as were her offspring; they murdered the weak and grew stronger by generation. The harvesters grew little by little until the scarce times were their greatest success. Preemptively culling the herd and ripping apart the weak before the hunters could find them and steal what was left.

Then he came. The moist one. It would have been easy to kill. But he stopped them. Echoing confusion in their brains until they lost sight or found another target.

Each time, he pushed harder, and the harvesters grew distracted. Food began to wander in. Confused and alive and warm. First, the slithering and crawling things, wet with filth and earth, but alive and warm. Next came the small furry things packed with protein that made them stronger. He favored the harvesters. The hunters were often gone and did not take interest in him. They returned to find the harvesters fed and strong. They began to pick over the scraps in the hard times. The harvesters favored him; they felt his power in their brains and the shivering flesh of the helpless meat that wandered into their nest. He had brought them. He provided, and the harvesters processed.

The big food began to wander in, and he was too soft and weak to feed himself. So, the harvesters began to bring him food in small bits. With his power, they grew, and with their power, the hunters waned. Starving and decrepit, they snuck the scraps of the beasts left behind, soaked in filth and the sticky, saliva-like enzymes the harvesters used to paralyze the meat. When he arrived, he pushed them to a tipping point, upsetting the order of the system, and it began to change rapidly.

Complex systems exhibit fat-tailed behavior. Not to be confused with a chaotic system. When describing chaos, a half-assed intellectual will chime in and give the book definition of a system in which minor changes in initial conditions lead to dramatic differences in outcomes. But this definition obviates the true nature of the system itself. In life, there are no initial conditions; every infinitesimal moment is the initial condition of the infinite moments that follow it. Fat-tailed behavior slightly improves upon this concept to account for the infinite. Simply stating that slight perturbations in the system lead to increasingly unpredictable and dramatic outcomes. It at least acknowledges the prior existence of the system and eliminates the need to attempt to define the initial conditions.

Just a slight push is all it takes. A new variable. A tipping point in the system that changes who gets the most protein. In animals, we acknowledge and study these fascinating systemic changes. In humans, we witness the end of the world as we know it and are terrified. So, were they terrified? Were the hunters terrified? When every slight shift is an existential threat, when hunger is the same as death, is there utility in fear? Is that fear where the soul resides? Perhaps the soul is nothing more than our contextualization of that fear. I have a powerful desire not to die, so there must be a reason to live.

∞ ∞ ∞

*The following is an excerpt from a notebook found under the bed of Cydnie Truth Devins by investigators on December 14th after he was reported missing:*

I tried to destroy this yesterday. Twice. Each time, I feel like these notes are a reminder and reinfection of my existence. Like they are the cause of my suffering, not just a product. The notebook itself has taken on a malicious tone in the way it resonates with the air. I tried tearing out pages first. I cried and threw them across the room. Trying to edit the past and future. But I stopped. Maybe this isn't a symptom or a cause, just a record. If I die today, will anyone ever know? Will the monster, or disease, or whatever the cause of this shared delusion go on unchallenged and unstoppable? I wonder if there have been others before me. If so, did they make it this far? So, I decided to try to repair the book. I taped the pages back inside and continued to scour the internet for anything I could find written by Stacey Travers. She is a journalist or blogger or something. But she knows. I can see it in her articles, but I found her real work online. The poetry, the descriptions, the darkness. She knows She sees what I see and perhaps more.

The second time I tried to destroy this notebook, I tried to burn it. I don't remember doing it, but when I coughed on the smoke and then realized where I was, I found it sitting face down on the gas stove. The alarm was going off, but I guess now I know it isn't networked. No one came to save me. When I got the alarm off, the room was silent, but for my coughing. I didn't feel better. Some of the record was gone. I can't remember how much; it all seems the same. Just some crispy sections of my saner first attempts at expressing this agony. Nothing sane remained. If this is a record, it's a poor one. The handwriting is only sometimes legible, sometimes in another language I don't fully understand yet. Sometimes, mindless doodles, sometimes visions of the horror in my dreams. But I'll keep doing it because, well, what the fuck else is there to do?

∞ ∞ ∞

I find myself hesitating. A moment's pause. A quiet second of solitude. Deciding if, after all this time, you are ready for the truth. It's a curious and simple word for a universal and particular feeling. A child lies by omission, a drunk weighs the risks of saying "no" or "I had a beer with dinner" to the stone-faced police officer on the side of the highway. Maybe if I continue to lie, I'll get away with it. On the other hand, honesty may garner favor. At the end of the day, we are betting agency for leniency. What is this but another form of submission? Agency, control, power, and freedom are synonyms. This leads us to the heart. Where does fear come from? A situation beyond your control? Or a situation you can control but fail to do so?

A rat submits slowly, panicking at first until it exhausts itself and gives up on life. Short bursts of adrenaline before the body collapses.

It's not just faith that drives you into that sort of thing.

More often than not.

A captain in a storm may put his faith in a god, but that only symbolizes accepting a chance of death, not accepting an inevitable death.

But you can't then argue that death itself is a universal fear.

A young warrior yearns for a glorious death in battle.

A Norse holmgang is voluntary, but through that glory is a brightness on the other side.

That promise is necessary.

That promise is hope.

But what lies at the far side of hope?

If technology obviates all pain, suffering and labor and effort, what is there remaining?

First of all, I won't pretend that I believe it is possible.

Humans are incapable of benefitting from their own efficiencies.

As we develop more efficient ways to hold meetings, do we increase free time?

No, we increase meetings.

As military equipment gets lighter and lighter with improved fabrics and designs, do soldiers benefit from the weight?

No, they carry more, lighter equipment.

And so, if we carry that verifiable logic on, there is no future in which humans have run out of things to do.

Regardless, let's pause a moment and consider a future in which artificial intelligence, networked autonomous vehicles, and other technologies have allowed humans to rid themselves of the need for production.

Nanotechnology has created a post-scarcity world, and no human goes without.

Would people embrace a life of leisure and suddenly live and let live?

Would global peace ensue?

We are smart animals, but animals, nonetheless.

The richest and most influential people still kill themselves, still have crises.

How would you measure yourself with nothing to differentiate you from your neighbor?

Religion wouldn't be required to explain the suffering of the world.

Would you measure yourself by your morality?

By your experiences?

By your parenting?

All of your social constructs, society itself, is a scaffolding upon which to measure your value.

Not to society, but your own perception of your self-worth.

Perhaps you would lash out in physical and psychological spasms, desperately trying to find your escape from the pit.

You are drowning.

You have to find purpose.

How long until you give up like the rat accepting its fate?

If the drowning rat had a gun, would it kill itself to get it over with?

What if it had a knife?

A rope?

A woodchipper?

It begs the question: how bad is despair?

To what lengths will we go to escape it?

Does it matter?

Can we measure suffering beyond the smiley-frowny face scale on the wall of the doctor's office?

What is the hopelessness face?

Neutral, I think.

You know?

People look blank; they look at you without really looking.

They don't see because they are looking past you, perhaps through into nothing.

In the bad moments, I would imagine bullet holes in the faces of every passerby I saw.

I fantasized about pinning down bystanders and punching them in the face until I felt the crunch of a zygomatic bone or my fist crumble into mush.

I imagined the metatarsals twisting and bursting through the skin and dangling by a bloody mess of tendons.

I looked at people; I saw death.

I wished pain and suffering on those around me.

Out of boredom, rage, despair, and lust, I felt nothing and everything.

Praying for my tongue to fall out and my eyes to explode.

At my worst moments, I felt it happen.

I knew it. I imagined hard enough, and it became real.

I stared at the apartments around me and climbed to the highest places I could.

Was that despair?

What about you?

What have you done that you've kept hidden from the world?

The dark secrets that drive us away from others.

We tuck them deep below the surface into the darkness.

But when you stare into the darkness, it stares right back.

And when it finds you, you don't get to walk away.

It's with you now, hulking over your every move.

Waiting, feeding, always feeding.

Is it in you now?

Did you find it here?

Unlikely. You brought it with you.

It's watching, always watching.

You can feel it caressing the back of your neck, and up your ears, like an imperceptible wind. A draft from nowhere, caressing your throat, whispering "danger" in your mind. You can see it. It lingers on the edges of sight. Just past the peripheral, just too deep in the shadows. You saw that movement; you sensed the malice. But it is gone. Just enough to make you doubt yourself. But your own horror lies within those confines. You can hear it. It lies in the mindless static of your room, the whir of electronics, fans, and the wiring in the walls. The zipper-hum of activity. It never leaves you. It lies in the forests, distant, scurrying things hiding from the silent killers. Wind rustles and shivers the life around you. But it's there too. It never leaves. Down, go down, always down. Down into the depths of your smallest closet, your deepest despair, your grave. Follow your thoughts to culmination. It's always death at the end.

But it just doesn't leave. You can run; you can ward it off with sex and drugs. You can hold it at bay for years with love and family. But it's waiting. It's an ancient thing that cares little for your greatest challenges.

∞ ∞ ∞

God I fucking hate this god I fucking hate this god I fucking hate this god I fucking hate this god I fucking hate this godifuckinghatethisgodifuckinghatethisgod i fucking hate this god i fucking hate this god. I fucking hate this god. I fucking hate this God. I fucking hate this God. I fucking hate this fuck I fucking hate this fucking god.

There is no end to this. It follows all.

∞ ∞ ∞

I found this book at the library yesterday. Copied here, just in case:

From *On the Societal Structures of Man and Beast: God and Chaos* by Mortimer Bronson, Ph.D., Page 147:

Indeed, one must hypothesize that hunting and gathering are two absolute truths of social enterprise. Society is not unique to man. Throughout his famous expeditions in Africa and the West Indies, Lord Hemmings, the second son of the famous explorer, traveled throughout Africa and South America in the early 1800s during his anthropological studies.

He was particularly fascinated by the complex yet simple nature of social organizations among species. Naturally, one could today argue that this is the very essence of zoological study in itself, but the young lord deviated from the norms of the time and was ostracized by his very taboo practice of comparing humanity to the beasts he studied. Today, we might call his earliest studies the precursor to complexity theory and agent-based modeling. Complex adaptive systems have existed for much longer than we have cared to characterize them as such, but the framework itself offers us a new window through which we seek to understand the universe.

In multiple species all over the world, organisms organize their societies into violent and non-violent roles. Some are warriors meant to defend from threats, others are hunters meant to gather resources. On the opposite side of the spectrum lay the non-violent roles, in their simplest form, often characterized by localized or passive resource collection such as farming or harvesting. They may also carry out such tasks as caring for the young or building shelter.

As the relative complexity of a species increases, so do these fundamental roles. Ants are assigned a role at birth and carry it out until death with no room for change. Some species divide roles along gender lines, and while Lord Hemming often cited these findings as a justification and evidence of the natural subservience of women (himself being a well-known misogynist), a closer look shows that societies throughout time and across the globe, to include humans, have assigned dissimilar roles to the genders. Many have even been more accepting of transgender and intersex members, who have existed in every species as a byproduct of biological life itself.

As societies continue to evolve in complexity, the rules become less binary, roles diversify, and some even become obsolete. For much of human society, violence has become less necessary altogether, and new roles emerge, such as "breadwinner" or "provider." Money becomes the new food. It is a substitute for the value of a fresh kill and the nutrition of the meat.

The main one that talks. He shows me. He shows me a great struggle between two deaths. But where do I fall into this? Why was I chosen? Is this some higher evil or meaningless coincidence? Has any of it happened at all?

∞ ∞ ∞

Nothing is all. Death is blind or incompetent. It never finds the willing. But perhaps the brave seek it out while the cowards lie in wait. Or beg for mercy.

I am stuck here in a corpse that isn't mine. I see its hands scurrying. I see its spelling errors. I feel its breath and its leaden heart. It heaves and gropes and imposes itself on the universe. It offends the senses. Would that I could peal it off. Take off the skin and reveal the inside. Open the chest into the soul and scrape off the rotten meat. Dig through the bones and squelching blood to find beauty, if there ever was any.

∞ ∞ ∞

Fuck that fucking hurts. I wish I could just throw it all up.

<u>If my letters were hieroglyphs.</u>

Woe to that advanced species,
Whether homegrown or traveler from afar,
Crouching over a small green book.
Probing with humming tools
Tinkering and preserving my ancient notes.

My Ms are inconsistent.

My Js are like Ss that had a stroke.
The size and angle vary letter by letter,
Word by word, thought by thought.
It almost looks like cursive.

Then again, it also looks like
A microwaved snake,
Or a spring that was run over by a train.

These future cryptologists
Dedicated their lives,
And professional reputations.
Carefully theorizing the
Grand, unified thoughts
That created my shopping list.

∞ ∞ ∞

Dear Diary,

Remember that time that I tried to cure my depression by smiling? I heard that the simple act of smiling could trick your body into releasing dopamine. A Pavlov thing, brain-body connection, and whatnot.

So, I would just smile. A big, cheesy grin. Until my jaw ached. I walked around like fucking Pennywise. It creeped people out. I drooled and cried, but I kept smiling. By the end, I threw up. The pain was too much. I wasn't better, that's it. No fucking story, no climax and denouement. Just a fucking dumb kid who turned into a dumb fucking adult.

The world could be quieter. I could just start killing people. I assume this is similar to what psychopaths go through before they snap. Do I have a breaking point? I wonder where it is.

∞ ∞ ∞

A great lie we tell ourselves. We are better off when we are cured. When we beat our addictions. Mental health is rooted in loneliness. Isolation. But it's not a simple loneliness that is cured with social interaction. It's a shaky foundation upon which we erect our crudely fastened lives. To be clean is to accept that you will be alone for the rest of your life. Even if you make friends, love family, get married, and have kids for whom you would die. It will always be there, just below the surface, ready to expose itself in a lull in conversation or a faded smile. To remind you, that this is what you are. Even if you make peace and like yourself in your cognitive brain. You will always be a little less.

Some burdens cannot be lifted; they can only be carried.

Now, here's the rub, though. We can carry anything. And I mean that. It's an encouraging thought. To kill yourself or others, you have to take action. Not like holding up a heavy weight or hanging onto a lover over the edge of a cliff. In those scenarios, the steady state is that the weight is dropped. Potential energy exists in the system, and it requires effort to prevent that natural state from happening. But at the end of the day, a human's steady state is not murder or suicide. It requires a decision and effort. So, no matter how much you feel that way, all you have to do to carry the burden is… nothing. It's there regardless of what you do.

I wonder if that is the core of religions with some more positive framing. Accepting you have no control relieves some of the burden. Must be nice

# COMING HOME

As a young man, I was eager to die
for a just cause, a good reason.
Contemplating a marker,
"die for anyone."
But when opportunity came and went
I paused and steadied my frozen desert feet
Teetering against the seismic shift.
And many years later, trudged into happiness.
Perhaps dying is the easy part.
Perhaps nobility is a veil over cowardice.
After all,
legacies only have value to the living.
--*Poem by James McLroy, unpublished.*

There's beauty in the suffering. Amid all of the cliches and social scaffolding meant to keep us afloat and out of despair. Purpose, love, faith. All our mechanisms to deal with pain are dedicated to its relief, its elimination, or at least its reduction. Pain is evil itself, and we dole out drugs, mantras, and candy to escape it.

But we rarely stop to admire it. The beauty in the struggle, in continuing to wake up. Instead, we perceive that beauty through art. Sad songs at the right moment don't necessarily make us happy, but they make suffering acceptable, even desirable. A broken, alcoholic saxophonist sipping whiskey at a wooden bar with the distorted light of a rain-soaked window behind him, looking out upon a dirty city where the people pass through silently, each with their own burdens and joys. He sits quietly with his thoughts, lingering on the loss of a fleeting love now gone. The thunder mumbles outside, reminding him of the warmth of the room, and he briefly overhears the giggles of a young couple in the corner sitting closer than mere friendship would allow. The young man's face is flushed as he desperately tries to find the words to make this moment last forever. But the musician sees only himself in the mirror. Their closeness is a reminder that he'll never find that connection again. Because the woman he'd died for beat him to it, leaving the world gray and absolute.

He finishes his drink and wonders politely when death will find him. Motions to the bartender and signs his check before turning to the heavy wooden door and casting himself back out into the soggy dark night.

There's beauty in the pain. Depression causes us to imagine ourselves differently: not happy, but resolute and unique. And that is enough for some. Some would rather die interesting than sacrifice it for belonging and happiness. No matter how many times we look up and see the pale, dead faces of the people around us, or how many times we dry heave over the toilet, desperate to get the feeling of perpetual heartbreak out of our systems like poison, some of us get up. And then we get up again.

Every day. Living in the beautiful suffering. Hating every moment but pitying those who haven't seen the same world. Pity and envy. Wishing desperately to be so naïve but secretly detesting those that are. Could you live with yourself being happy without forgetting the suffering of the world and the dark shadows in your past?

The truth knowers, the seers of the world, are alone. For even to find each other, humans can't communicate knowledge so vastly beyond our biology. The feeling, the real, pure, unfiltered feeling, cannot be described with words. Language itself is a filter. Even the choice of words must consider the audience, so we can't choose the words we want. If they don't resonate with the audience, the communication has failed. If we change our words to resonate, the communication has failed. It must be translated and simplified. Coded for transmission, then decoded. And there will always be so much lost in translation. We know each other; we sense each other. In a crowded room, listening to a group introduce themselves, I'll already know who I want to talk to. Why have they always tried to kill themselves? Suffering makes you interesting? Am I becoming more empathetic or nihilistic?

∞ ∞ ∞

*I found her after sitting comfortably for hours. Sitting below the scene, feeling grateful and briefly happy. I wanted the break. I needed the break. While it all decayed. What if I had come back earlier?*

The silence hung in the air like fog. So oblivious, so blind, talking to myself. Coming home from work, all I could think of was my own fatigue. Another day of grey. Short-cut carpets that hide stains, grey cubicle walls, and neutral-toned desks. Muffled conversations from across the room "...hardly working..."

"How's it going?"

"Still standing, what more can you ask for, right? How about you?"

"Can't complain, I mean, no one would listen if I did!"

Muffled and forced laughter. In those cubicles, it's hard to tell if they're one room over or a mile away. The sound is so suffocating. The air of the room pressed against my weary skin through collar stays and wool blazers. Every day felt like life itself was trying to kill me, squeezing and squeezing. I shuffled around a grey office, doing what needed to be done, avoiding eye contact. Reveling in the short respite from the worse challenges waiting at home and chastising myself for doing so.

It wasn't the others' fault; they'd reach out and try to connect. "What are you doing this weekend?" they'd ask. I'd lie and pretend that I never thought that far ahead, but I dreaded the conversation. I hid in my work so I wouldn't have to talk about my home or about anything at all. Thoughts always lingering on what she said. The day before, or was it last week? Sometimes, years-old blow-ups and breakdowns. The constant balance between defending myself and trying to pry the blame from her. She always blamed me until I won the argument, and then she broke down and abused herself so much that I argued my way back into being at fault.

*What if I had been earlier?* So, I hopelessly teetered and balanced and panicked through the day, never knowing who would be asleep with me in my bed tonight. Who would be waiting for me when I came home?

I became obsessed with the fear, tiptoeing for some misguided sense of control or caring. Measuring my self-worth through emotional endurance. I was tired; I was always tired. Always searching for a light or escape that never came. That day, the drive home was silent, like most days. I had forgotten how long my commute was. *Was I driving slower than usual? Did I take comfort in the red lights?* Seconds, minutes, and hours had little meaning in my internal perceptive reality. Thought flowed, coalesced, and dissolved in a seamless fashion, and I teleported to my home.

∞ ∞ ∞

Home. After a long day, the crunch of the door echoing across the parking lot. I pause just a moment to breathe the fall air. Fresh with decaying leaves. The sun had already moved behind the row of houses, but the pavement glowed with its leftover heat. *What if I had rushed in? Would it have been fast enough?*

Up the steps to the door. The key, but wait, the door is unlocked. I moved inside into the tight foyer. *I knew something was wrong, but I didn't check the house. Would it have been soon enough?*

"Hey, babe!" I echo into the wooden chamber. No reply. I sighed slightly in relief... relief. I can have my moment of peace. A moment I rarely received after

Ophie was born. I would call and see where Rebecca had gone, but after a beer and a moment to myself.

Removing shoes, feeling the cool air and release from the compression of my day, washing my face in the kitchen sink and grabbing a beer from the refrigerator. Feeling the cool floor through my dress socks. That irreplaceable feeling of your toes spreading for the first time all day. Maybe I should stop standing so much. Nah, my back still spasms whenever I sit at a desk. Ah well.

Setting the cold glass bottle on the counter, I twist my torso until my spine releases that crunchy and familiar crack. Releasing some of the pressure on my neck. A little more relief, and I can finally sit down. I never just watch TV anymore. Falling into the couch and digging in the seat cushions for the remote. Finding it, feet up on the coffee table, and flipping through shows.

I feel it, like a yawn, a deep breath stretching out the stress from my chest after a long week. The first inkling of relaxation in months. My cheeks tighten into a very amateur smile. The screen goes dark, leaving only my pasty face staring back at me. And suddenly, I am confronted with my selfishness. 'I better call Rebecca. Or at least get dinner started.'

I text Rebecca. "Hey babe, home, where you at?" and shut off the TV. Heading toward the kitchen to check the list of our chosen meals.

Washing rice, over and over, until the water runs clear. Over and over, fill, swirl, pour. Fill, swirl, pour. Why was there so much starch in this batch? Fill, swirl, pour.

Next, onions. I have always liked cutting onions, not for the pain but for simple organization. If you cut it just right, it cooks just right.

Still no word. She never waits this long to respond. Better call.

The phone is heavy in my hand.

I see the cracks along the outside of the case and the cool back from lying on the counter.

A brief pause as the phone rings.

Nothing... nothing.

Then I hear it, that haunting buzz.

The cheery ring from upstairs.

She left her phone. She never leaves her phone.

She's done it; she's left me. But where is the baby?

The house rotates and glides beneath me. I stop breathing, and I am at the base of the stairs.

"Babe? You home?"

Still no breathing. Fire scalds my stomach lining. The house sinks beneath me, and I levitate up the steps.

The ringing ceases, leaving the echoes stinging the air.

I find my feet coated suddenly in lead. I take heavy steps, straining against the weight.

Halfway up, I hear it. Faintly echoing off the hallway walks

*Drip, drip, drip.*

At the top of the stairs, I see the dark stain of water saturating the hall carpet.

*Drip, drip, drip.*

Death is blue.

Blue and white.

Blue and white and fat.

I pull my baby from the tub.

Desperately pressing with my crossed fingers.

Minutes, hours, years.

I hear the tin voice of the operator grating through the phone like sandpaper.

"911, what's your emergency?"

Did I dial them?

What did I say?

She killed my baby.

She killed our daughter.

Why did she kill my daughter?

I screamed, I whispered, I fought as they pulled me away.

I had no life; she took my life.

She killed me too, and I was blue and white and bloated from the water.

Pain and anger so strong she split into two people.

One I mourned, and one I wanted to kill.

But the baby.

The baby who never was.

The baby.

My daughter.

I felt happiness so briefly, sitting on the couch six feet below the corpse of my daughter. How can I continue to live? Death would relieve my suffering. There is beauty and justice in the suffering.

∞ ∞ ∞

Bathing in white light. This was different from Cyd's usual dreams.

*"It's okay, Cyd. You're safe now."* A warm voice, Rebecca's voice, echoed in his mind.

"Becca"

*"It's okay, Cyd. You're safe now. We all are."*

"Becca, this isn't real. You're dead."

*"Fair enough, but here I am talking to you."*

"How is that? Am I dead?"

*"No. Not dead, not yet. But you're safe. For now. You need to do something for me."*

"I can't imagine why I would do anything for you. You killed her. Fuck you!"

*"You don't mean that. No, I saved her. You, if no one else, should understand that. You can hear him too. He's getting stronger. You can't put it out of your mind because you know it's true."*

"I don't know what the fuck it is. It sure as hell isn't Satan or some fucking demon. It's just our problem. Depression or schizophrenia or something."

*"There's no hallucination with depression..."*

"Sometimes there is!"

*"There's no shared hallucination in schizophrenia."*

"God, fuck off. You aren't even real. You don't know. Some new brain disease? Some brain-eating bacteria or amoeba? There are a bunch of possibilities and you decided to go with the easy one. 'Oh no, Satan is after my soul.' How fucking unimaginative."

*"You're wrong."*

"And you took her with you. It wasn't enough that I have to live with failing you. You took her. How can anyone go on like this?"

*"What else is there to do. You could go down to the dark places. You could seek him out. You could seek him out. You could go down."*

"What did you say?"

*"You could go down. Isn't that what he is always saying? Go down."*

"Why would you want that if you think he'll take my soul? What does it even mean anyway?"

*"I... don't want it. You want it. Prove me wrong or something? Either way. Peace will come to you eventually."*

"You've changed. Maybe it's my subconscious warping your memory. I've loved and hated you for so long now, I don't know what you are anymore."

*"I'm your wife. I love you. And I'm not dead. I'm eternal."*

"Bullshit."

*"Why do you still doubt?"*

"There is no doubt. Doubt requires effort. There is no order, there is no meaning. We exist as the result of millennia of entropy and interactions between nodes governed by physics."

*"Always with this crap. How can you be so sure."*

"Because everything else is governed by it. Through suffering. Either you are evil, or I am according to your rules. By any measure, the outcome is the same. What does it matter what you believe. No amount of purpose will attenuate the misery you've caused."

*"You can come down. It's comfortable here."*

"SHUT UP! God, how can I even be so riled up by my own projection of you."

*"Probably because you can't control your anger toward me."*

"Maybe."

*"Cydnie?"*

"What."

*"If this was a dream, wouldn't you have woken up by now?"*

"Lucid dreams exist. Who knows? They don't all have to be thrilling."

*"Well, then try to wake up."*

"I am."

*"But you can't. Doesn't that seem odd?"*

"Your voice sounds weird."

*"How so?"*

"Deeper, more menacing."

*"You can be such a drama queen."*

...

"You're not her, are you?"

*"Of course I am me. The only reason I'm here is to tell you to come with me."*

"I'm not going to kill myself."

*"Then don't. Go find him. He'll just keep killing if you don't."*

"After all of this terror that drove you to murder your own child, you want me to go find him?"

*"It's not my fault, it's his. Maybe you're right; I'm not me. I'm a projection of your subconscious. I'm only telling you what you already know but are too stubborn to realize. Just go down. Down to the darkness, and you'll find him."*

"How? There is so much darkness."

*"Others have found him. There are no mountain lions in Cambridge Cyd."*

"How do you know that?"

*"I don't, you know it."*

"The blogger?"

*"Yes, the sweet blogger."*

"How can I find her?"

*"Find her and come down."*

"I will. But you're not Becca."

*"Come down and find us. We're here and we're safe and we need help, and we don't have long."*

"You're him."

*"I'm you. There is no him here. Find the writers, find the seers, and you will find him."*

"You're him... you did this to me."

*"I do nothing. I feed."*

"You took her from me. You took them both."

*"I take nothing. They find me. You find me. It's alright. Come find me. I need help. I don't have much time."*

What the hell are you talking about?

*"Help me. Help. Me. Come down. Feed me. COME FIND US."*

Cyd's eye opened to dusty rays of light from his half-covered windows. He lay on his side in a cold puddle on the mattress. A brown stain flowed from the nearly empty bottle of whiskey in his right hand all the way down to the valley he created with his body weight. A headache hovered above his skull. The kind that threatened to crash down on top of him at the slightest movement. He wanted to go back to sleep. But a chill came over him. Why? What the hell was he dreaming about? It was Becca, as usual. But what was she saying? She turned into something. Something different. Or perhaps she was never Becca at all. Sickness plunged into his stomach and bones, and he rushed to the bathroom to vomit. Coughing and retching, he heard the voice again. *"Come down. It's safe and warm. Come to the dark places and help us."*

It was in his dreams now too. It started as intrusive thoughts. Annoying but harmless. Then came the daydreams and the out-of-body experiences and hallucinations. It was not going to get better. It was getting worse. He lay on his back, feeling the cold tiles on his bare skin. He needed water, lots of it, and fast. So, he started by lurching forward onto his knees and turning on the shower before collapsing back to the ground. On the counter above him, he saw the torn edge of a plastic baggie peak over the edge and the glint of white powder residue illuminated by the sunlight from the next room.

'When the fuck did I get molly?' He shuddered with a chuckle and began to cry. The next day would be rough. People always said molly and ecstasy withdrawal made you depressed, but it was more nuanced. He lost emotional regulation and wafted cyclically between euphoria, despair, and intense, aggressive arousal, like his brain was trying to catch its balance. He closed his eyes and felt the warm tears begin to pass over his temples and slide down to his ears and the floor.

When he woke, the sunlight shifted. The counter was no longer illuminated, and the mirror dripped with steam. He hoped it was only a short doze. Next came the body aches, but he pulled his lame corpse over the edge of the tub and lay there until his fingers were soggy. A shower had a way of helping and harming at the same time. Like debriding a burn wound. Stripping away the damage to begin the healing process.

He had to find the writer. The one who had been making those weird posts. It wasn't much, but this wouldn't stop otherwise.

Balancing on one foot.
Not even, just the ball while
anxiously wriggling toes against
the ground. They're bound to break.
They must break.

Yearning to be tentacles,
grasping the head of a beam
that suspends us thousands,
(no, millions) of feet above the ground
(if there is even a ground).

And it occurs to me,
Perhaps there is no ground.
No sudden stop at the bottom.
Cons of fear anchored to nothing.
A dangling anchor leaving us forever straining

against the turning of the world.
What happens if we just. Stop?
And pitch ourselves backward into redemption.
I'm sure the weight gets easier.
Terror numbs the pain.

# SIMULATING CHANGE STRATEGY

MERGING STAKEHOLDER
MANAGEMENT AND BASS DIFFUSION
By: Harriet M. Sackler

## INTRODUCTION:

### Background

Change theory endeavors to describe and define the ways in which humans execute and cope with changes. This critical field crosses multiple sectors as leaders attempt to develop organizations that are fatalistically set in their ways. Unfortunately, because of the inherent complexity of human interactions on an organizational scale, there are few reliable "laws" that managers can put into a "tool kit" and expect consistent results. This study is an exploration into developing such a tool by answering the following questions:

1. Can Bass diffusion simulate change within an organization?

2. How can system dynamics model change theory within organizations?

3. How can organizational leaders use diffusion modeling to manage change?

The purpose of this study is to examine organizational change theory using an adaptation of the Bass diffusion model. The study simplifies and quantifies variables and processes involved in change. It also outlines relationships between variables that leaders and managers can consider when leading change within their organizations.

# LITERATURE REVIEW

<u>Complex Adaptive Systems Literature: Bass Diffusion</u>
The study of innovation diffusion began with the recognition that thoughts and rumors spread through populations similarly to infectious diseases. Frank Bass first modified the logistic model to account for the spontaneous adoption of innovations, but his model has become widely used and adapted across disciplines.[1] Scholars have recognized the potential of diffusion modeling in organizational change, though there are few practical decision-making tools to come from the body of research. A study by Kheseoul Kim found that while organizations benefit from insights of diffusion research, they "rarely take advantage of notions and methodologies of diffusion research when developing

---

[1] James E. Sterling, *Business Dynamics: Complexity and Systems Thinking for Sharks,* (Boston, MA: McGraw-Hill Companies, Inc., 2000), 332.

their own frameworks."[2] In 2002, Shawna Abbington, a Professor at George Mason University, failed to account for this phenomenon but did acknowledge a possible reason for this disconnect. In an article in *New Directions for* Evaluation, she described diffusion as a model of change that "focuses on individual decision making" and argued that it was, therefore, unfit for usage in macro-evaluation of organizational change.[3] While it is often applied to organizations, it remains, at its core, a discussion about person-to-person transfer. Until the development of computers and simulation software, it was likely an intimidating task to apply seemingly "micro" concepts to the "macro" world of large organizations. This is especially true due to the apparent differences in skill sets and interests of those who spend their careers in business and those who study system dynamics.

## Organizational Change Theory

Change theory is a diverse brand of social science dominated by multiple differing theorists and models. It is conducted primarily through what Donald Goldstein called "practice-based research," based on putting hypotheses into action and recording the results.[4] Some key theories considered for this project were Kurt Lewin's "unfreeze-transition-freeze" model, John

---

2 Kheseoul Kim, "Organizational diffusion of changes," *Organizational Change Management*, Vol. 18, Issue 2, (2005) , 135.
3 Shawna R. Abbington, "Evaluation implications of innovation diffusion," *New Directions for Evaluation*, Vol. 2002 No. 263, 105-115.
4 "Emotional Leadership" presented by Donald Goldstein, Harvard Kennedy School of Government, Cambridge, MA, October 18, 2003.

Kotter's 8-Step model for change, and the United States Army's "Leading Change Process."[5]

Many theories include stakeholder management, but there is no established consensus about how the individual affects the organizational change process. The Kotter and Army models most closely codify the role of individuals through a "guiding coalition."[6] Kotter argues that long-term change can only be successful through the actions of a team with the "right composition and sufficient trust among members."[7] Likewise, the Army focuses on building a core group of change champions that will lead the change in the organization.[8] Therein lies a research gap. While most major change theorists agree that individual attitudes toward change are critical to the success or failure of that change, there is little theory or technique for evaluating these effects. To this point, the closest that the current body of knowledge provides is a loose definition of types of agents within the organization based on their attitudes toward change.

This guiding coalition is broken down in other works throughout change management theory to classify types of individuals based on their attitude toward change. While the titles used vary slightly throughout different

---

[5] Kurt Lewin. "Frontiers in group dynamics: Concept, method and reality in social science; social equilibria and social change." *Human Relations*, 1947, 34-35.; John Kotter. *Leading Change*. (Boston, MA: Harvard Business School Press, 1996), 21.; Headquarters, Department of the Army, *Army Doctrine Publication (ADP) 6-22: Army Leadership and the Profession*, (Washington, DC: Department of the Army, 2009), 9-2.
[6] John Kotter. *Leading Change.*, 51.
[7] Ibid., 55.
[8] "L104: Leading Organizations in Change" presented by LTC Johnathan Williamson, The Command and General Staff College, Fort Leavenworth, KS, September 19, 2001.

theories, the definitions remain largely the same. For the purposes of this study, the researcher chose a common four-element framework:

Champions - Individuals are classified as "Champions" who lead change. They take ownership of the proposed organizational changes and act independently to bring them about either through formal or informal authorities. The change champions make up what the Army calls the guiding coalition.

Supporters – Change supporters passively encourage change but do not take an active role in bringing it about. They may publicly or privately support the change, but if left to their own devices, they would remain in the status quo.

Bystanders – As the name implies, bystanders have a neutral attitude towards change. They do not care enough to support or resist the change.

Resisters – Resisters actively seek to prevent the change from happening. They may do so publicly or privately, but without a guiding coalition and enough institutional effort, resisters will dismantle the organizational change effort from within.[9]

# RESEARCH METHODOLOGY

Analysis Framework

---

[9] Global Tech World, *Change Theory – The Basics*, November 9, 2009, 7. https://accelerationprograms.edu/assets/files/trainingaids/1743364/globaltechwor ld2011_change-theory-the-basics_en.pdf.

This study utilized a stock and flow model of Bass diffusion and added a "turnover rate" to simulate the constant change in personnel within the system (figure 1). The researcher chose a stock and flow model for its simplicity. This decision came at the cost of precision. An agent-based model would have more appropriately included the relative power of agents in the organization and eliminated some assumptions made. However, an agent-based model would have been less accessible to leaders trying to plan change within their organizations. The purpose of this study is to provide a framework for leaders without training in system dynamics. The outcome must be simple to explain and understand for wider consumption. Therefore, a stock and flow model was more appropriate as it trades precision for utility.

The model makes assumptions about constants but remains flexible enough to adjust based on the conditions. Each change-agent category influences the adoption fraction. Once all the effects are calculated, their sum is adjusted by the popularity modifier, which accounts for the general popularity of the change. Any of these constants can be adjusted by the user based on their perceived or measured needs in their situation. The researcher ran the simulation multiple times while adjusting independent variables to make observations about the interactions between variables. Independent variables in this study were the ratios of change agents, the champion modifier, the resister modifier, the ad effectiveness, and the popularity. The researcher then compared the effects of each of these changes to draw conclusions.

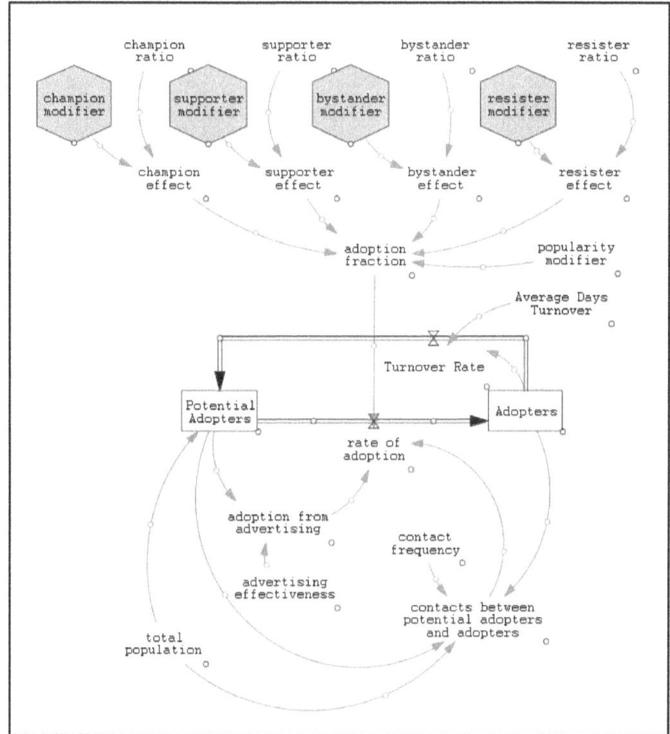


Figure 1. Visual Representation of the Hybrid Model

## Assumptions

Ratios of change agents. Ratios of types of change agents within an organization will change constantly based on the culture, climate, and issues the organization is facing. This model starts with a base case of 10% champions, 10% supporters, 60% bystanders, and 20% resisters.[10] Obtaining real-time, accurate ratios of change agents is likely impossible for this type of model. An

---

[10] Global Tech World, *Change Theory – The Basics*, November 9, 2009, 9.

agent-based model may provide further insights in the future.

Change agent modifiers. Modifiers represent the number of people per day that a change agent can convince to adopt the change. The base assumptions for these modifiers were: Champions: +.75, Supporters: +.5, Bystanders: +0, Resisters: -.6. These numbers would represent an aggregate in this system. Individual agent factors such as charisma, focus, formal and informal authority, and physical position within the organization will all have an effect on the modifiers in practice.

Organizational turnover. This model assumes that people enter and exit the organization at approximately the same rate, keeping the total population of the organization static. The model also assumes that personnel entering the organization have the same rate of adoption as those who were already in the organization. This turnover rate also incorporates a 14-day delay to simulate the time spent onboarding and integrating new personnel into an organization. These factors would have to be adjusted by the individual organization in order to improve the predictive accuracy of the model.

Importantly, there is an artificial and arbitrary slowdown to improve the readability of results. Once the adoption fraction is calculated, the model divides it by four. This must be removed when using the model for empirical work in which the time is relevant to decision-making. For the purposes of this study, the slowdown allows the researcher to make observations about the interactions between variables without affecting the interactions themselves.

## **DATA ANALYSIS**

### Results

The researcher ran the simulation under 51 different conditions, manipulating five variables in isolation. Each individual simulation is called a "run." Runs were recorded to analyze their subsequent effects on the dependent variables: number of potential adopters (P) and adopters (A), contacts between P and A, and rate of adoption. The independent variables studied were:

Ratios of Agent Types (base)
Advertising Effectiveness (adef)
Champion Modifier (cmod)
Resister Modifier (rmod)
Popularity Modifier (popularity)

### Ratios of Agent Types

The base set of runs manipulated the ratios of change agents to determine how each agent affected the overall adoption pattern. The simulations showed an exponential increase in the rate of adoption as the ratio of champions and supporters to resisters increases and vice versa (figure 2). Furthermore, the rate of adoption changes significantly when only minor adjustments are made to ratios; these effects change based on the efficacy of the agent modifiers.

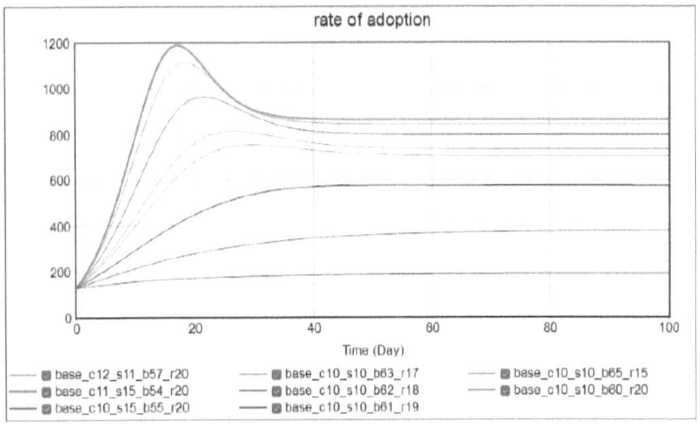

Figure 2. Rate of Adoption with Adjusted Ratios of Change Agent Types

### Advertising Effectiveness

Increasing the Advertising Effectiveness of the original Bass Diffusion model resulted in a constant increase in the rate of adoption (figure 3). However, even an extreme increase in effectiveness only led to a total adopter population of approximately half of the total population (figure 4). Simply put, how members of the organization felt about the change had a much stronger impact on adoption than the organization's ability to increase awareness of the change through outside means. "Word-of-mouth" was more powerful than "posting signs."

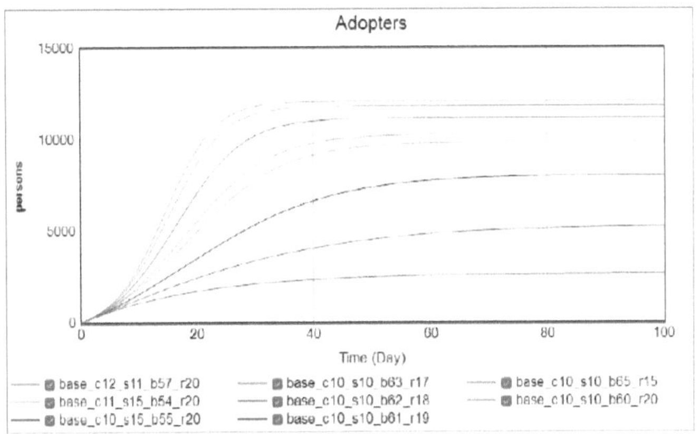

Figure 3. Total Adopters (out of 16,000) with Adjusted Ratios of Change Agent Types

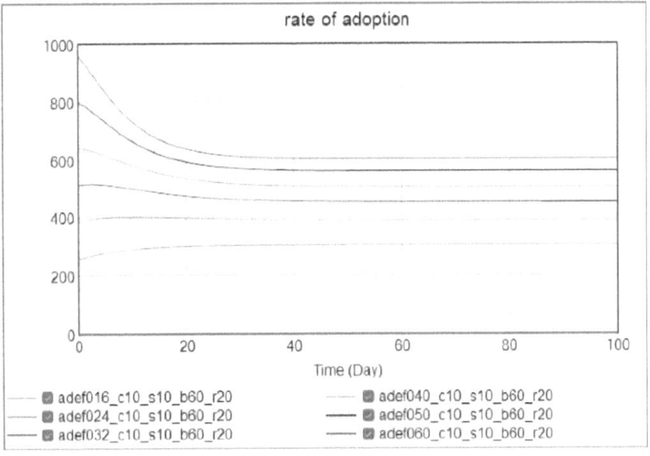

Figure 4. Rate of Adoption with Adjusted Advertising Effectiveness

## Champion and Resister Modifiers

Decreasing the champion modifier slowed the rate of adoption (figure 5), which decreased the number of adopters (figure 6). Adjusting the resister modifier generated mirroring effects. This reflects the nature of the adoption fraction as a function of a ratio of all agent effects. As mentioned above, agent-based modeling may provide further insights into the individual modifiers variable. This accounts for a multitude of individual characteristics such as Champion/Resister charisma, popularity, informal authority, pettiness, oratory skill, and others.

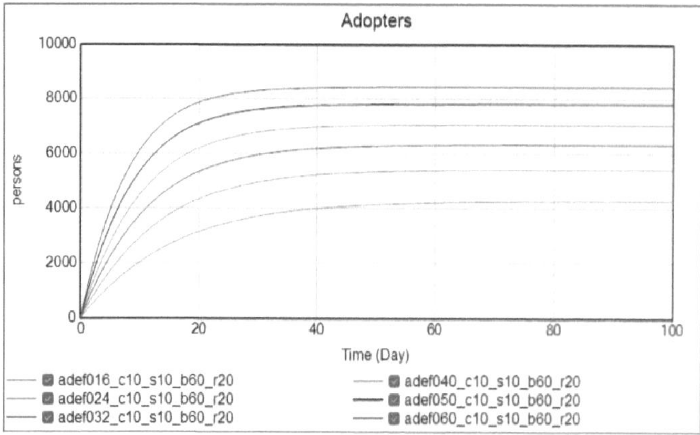


Figure 5. Total Adopters (out of 16,000) with Adjusted Advertising Effectiveness

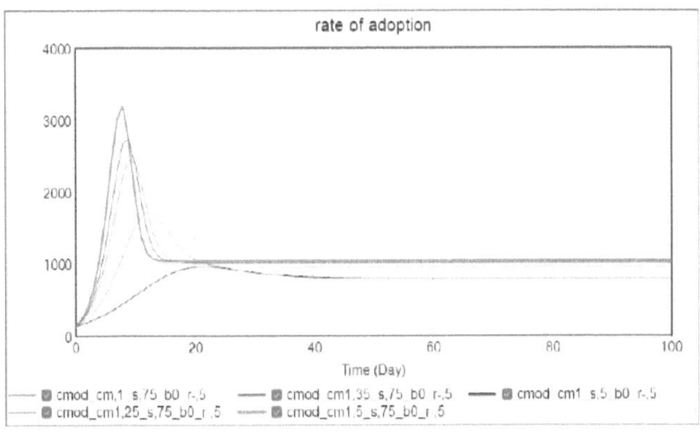



Figure 6. Rate of Adoption with Adjusted Champion Modifier

## Popularity Modifier

The popularity modifier adjusts the calculated adoption fraction based on the popularity of the change. The popularity modifier lies between 0 and 2 to ensure that popular and unpopular changes affect the output at the same magnitude. Simulations showed that popularity linearly increased or decreased the total ending stocks of adopters (figure 7). Like advertising effectiveness, this had a minor effect relative to the exponential effects of adjusting the ratios of change agents. This may have unintentionally made a statement on the inconsequentiality of preconceived opinions. Potential adopters may go into work with a decision on whether or not they will support a change, only to have it easily changed by a charismatic champion or resister.

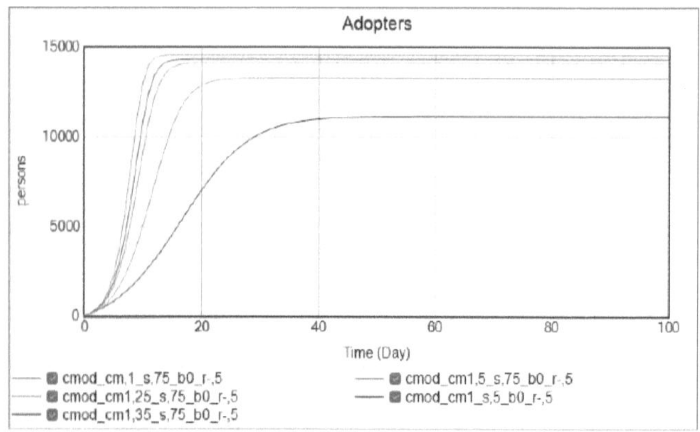



Figure 7. Total Adopters (out of 16,000) with Adjusted Champion Modifier

## Findings

The most dramatic results came from slight manipulations of the ratios of change agents. By converting relatively insignificant amounts of bystanders into supporters, the adoption fraction increased significantly. Each increase in the rate of adoption led to an increase in the total adopters within the system because the turnover rate remained constant.

Increasing the effectiveness of advertising was an ineffective method of increasing the rate of adoption. It is exceedingly difficult to measure and only resulted in just over 50% of total adoption (figure 4), even after increasing the effectiveness from .008 to .06. Popularity showed comparable results.

Adjusting the champion and resister modifiers showed the summative nature of the champion and supporter effects. If the sum of the champion and supporter effects (figure 1) is greater than the resister effect, the change will diffuse until the system reaches equilibrium. It is important to note, however, that due to the constant organizational turnover and balancing effect of incoming personnel's preconceived attitudes toward change, the organization never reaches a tipping point and, thus, never achieves 100% adoption.

# CONCLUSIONS AND RECOMMENDATIONS

### Summary of Results

The research showed that building a guiding coalition of champions and supporters more significantly affected total adoption than other factors. For example, increasing champions by 2% and supporters by 1% resulted in 2000 more total adopters than when advertising effectiveness increased by 750%. Even acknowledging this model's multiple assumptions, the interactions between variables suggest that organizational leaders have the greatest effect when focusing their time on their people, as opposed to advertising the change.

### Recommendations

Organizational leaders should actively research their organization's culture and needs before initiating a change process. This model serves as one option to explore and identify leverage points upon which to act to execute change. By manipulating the independent variables of this model, a manager can also estimate the progression of an organizational change and establish milestones. Should you assemble a bigger core of champions? Or will a culture supportive of change suffice? Should you focus on reducing resister efficacy by communicating the merits of the change? Or should you reduce resister numbers through disciplinary or administrative action? This model allows leaders to explore their options.

Some relationships merit further study. Adaptations to this model or wholly novel studies should ask some additional questions: how can a leader increase the efficacy of their champions? To what degree is a person's attitude toward change fixed? Does a person change freely between the four categories?

## Concluding Thoughts

After concluding the quantitative analysis, it is critical to remember the purpose of this model: to provide leaders with new perspectives as they lead change. Therefore, one must consider which independent variables are easily acted upon in the real world. A leader cannot reliably design new ways to advertise that dramatically increase its efficacy. Nor can the leader magically make a change more popular. However, a good leader can affect their change agents through daily interactions and leadership practices. By creating a culture open to new experiences or by establishing a "sense of urgency," a leader can change bystanders into supporters.[11] By communicating a vision and strategy to your team and empowering them with responsibility, the leader can turn supporters into champions. Simulations

---

[11] Kotter, J.P., *Leading Change*, 21.

such as this will not replace the need for leadership, but they can enhance the leadership skills available.

# APPENDIX A:
## Model Equations and Variables

### Adopters:

Definition: Persons who have adopted the desired change.

Equation: Adopters = INTEG (rate of adoption-Turnover Rate, 0)

Units: persons

### Adoption Fraction:

Definition: The likelihood that contact between a potential adopter and an adopter will result in adoption.

Equation: adoption fraction = ((champion effect + supporter effect + bystander effect + resister effect)/4) * popularity modifier

Units: none

### Adoption from Advertising:

Definition: The rate at which Potential Adopters will adopt based on advertising.

Equation: adoption from advertising = Potential Adopters * advertising effectiveness

Units: persons

### Advertising Effectiveness: (base value):

Definition: The likelihood that a potential adopter will adopt based on advertising.

Equation: advertising effectiveness = 0.008

Units: none

## Average Days Turnover:

Definition:  The number of days it takes to integrate a new person into the organization after an adopter leaves.

Equation:  Average Days Turnover = 14

Units:  days

## Bystander Effect:

Definition:  The cumulative effect that bystanders have on the adoption fraction.

Equation:  bystander effect = bystander ratio * bystander modifier

Units:  none

## Bystander Modifier (base value):

Definition:  The number of persons/day that a bystander will convince to adopt.

Equation:  bystander modifier = 0

Units:  persons/day

## Bystander Ratio (base value):

Definition:  Ratio of bystanders to total population.

Equation:  bystander ratio = 0.6

Units:  none

## Champion Effect:

Definition:  The cumulative effect that champions have on the adoption fraction.

Equation:  champion effect = champion modifier * champion ratio

Units:  persons/day

## Champion Modifier (base value)

Definition:  The number of persons/day that a champion will convince to adopt.

Equation:  champion modifier = .75

Units:  persons/day

## Champion Ratio (base value):

Definition:  Ratio of champions to total population.

Equation:  champion ratio = 0.1

Units:  none

## Contact Frequency:

Definition:  The average number of persons that each person comes into contact with per day.

Equation:  contact frequency = 30

Units:  persons/person/Day

## Contacts Between Potential Adopters and Adopters:

Definition:  Number of contacts that occur between a potential adopter and an adopter per day

Equation:  contacts between potential adopters and adopters = Potential Adopters * contact frequency * (Adopters/total population)

Units:  persons/persons/day

## Popularity Modifier (base value):

Definition:  Adjustment variable to account for differences in the popularity of changes.

Equation:  popularity modifier = 1

Units:  none

## Potential Adopters:

Definition: Persons who have not adopted the desired change.

Equation: Potential Adopters= INTEG (Turnover Rate - rate of adoption, total population)

Units: persons

## Rate of Adoption:

Definition: The number of persons per day that potential adopters are adopting the change.

Equation: rate of adoption = contacts between potential adopters and adopters * adoption fraction + adoption from advertising

Units: persons/day

## Resister Effect:

Definition: The cumulative effect that resisters have on the adoption fraction.

Equation: resister effect = resister modifier * resister ratio

Units: persons/day

## Resister Modifier (base value):

Definition: The number of persons/day that a resister will convince to adopt.

Equation: resister modifier = -.6

Units: persons/day

## Resister Ratio (base value):

Definition: Ratio of resisters to total population.

Equation: resister ratio = 0.2

Units: none

**Supporter Effect:**

Definition:  The cumulative effect that supporters have on the adoption fraction.

Equation:  supporter effect = supporter modifier * supporter ratio

Units:  persons/day

**Supporter Modifier (base value):**

Definition:  The number of persons/day that a supporter will convince to adopt.

Equation:  supporter modifier = 0.5

Units:  persons/day

**Supporter Ratio:**

Definition:  Ratio of bystanders to total population.

Equation:  supporter ratio = 0.1

Units:  none

**Total Population:**

Definition:  The total number of persons in the organization.

Equation:  total population = 16,000

Units:  persons

**Turnover Rate:**

Definition:  The number of persons/day that leave the organization and are replaced by new personnel.

Equation:  Turnover Rate = Adopters / Average Days Turnover

Units:  persons/day

# **APPENDIX B:**
## **Tables**

| ID # | Run Name | Cham. (%) | Supp. (%) | Byst. (%) | Resi. (%) | Days to reach max change | Steady Ratio of Adoption (%) |
|---|---|---|---|---|---|---|---|
| R1 | base_c12_s11_b57_r20 | 12 | 11 | 57 | 20 | 50 | 64 |
| R2 | base_c11_s15_b54_r20 | 11 | 15 | 54 | 20 | 47 | 76 |
| R3 | base_c10_s15_b55_r20 | 10 | 15 | 55 | 20 | 47 | 70 |
| R4 | base_c10_s10_b63_r17 | 10 | 10 | 63 | 17 | 53 | 61 |
| R5 | base_c10_s10_b62_r18 | 10 | 10 | 62 | 18 | 72 | 50 |
| R6 | base_c10_s10_b61_r19 | 10 | 10 | 61 | 19 | 33 | 93 |
| R7 | base_c10_s10_b65_r15 | 10 | 10 | 65 | 15 | 40 | 74 |
| R8 | base_c10_s10_b60_r20 | 10 | 10 | 60 | 20 | 92 | 17 |

Table 1. Ratio Manipulation Runs

# <u>APPENDIX C: Additional Figures</u>

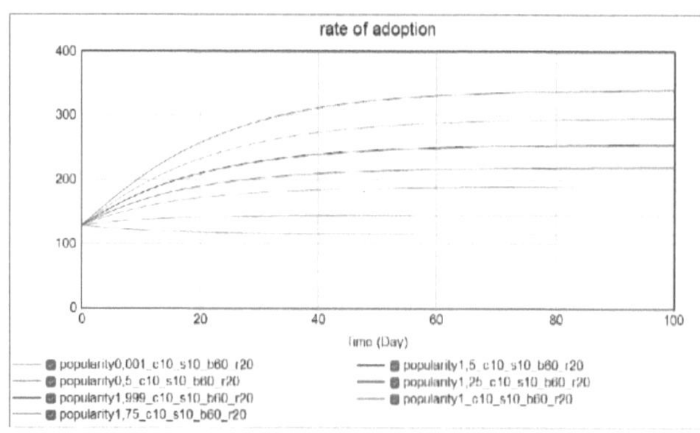

Figure 8. Rate of Adoption with Adjusted Popularity

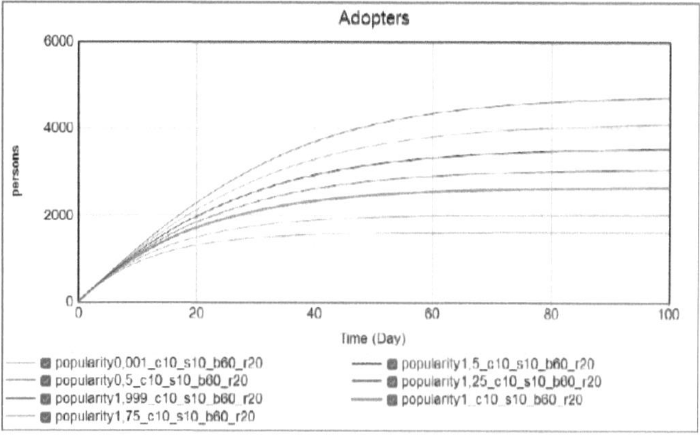

Figure 9. Total Adopters (out of 16,000) with Adjusted Popularity

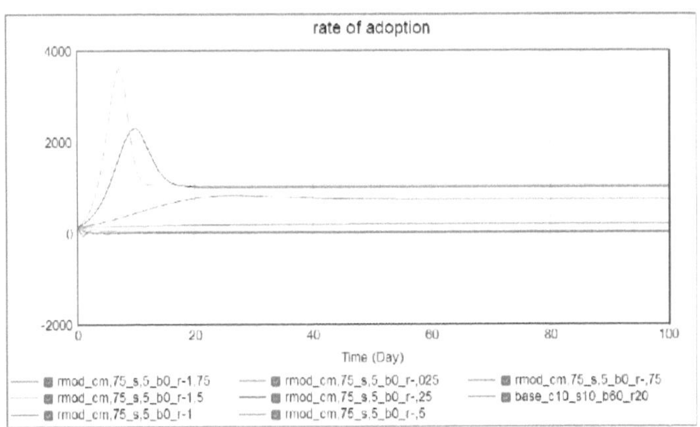

Figure 10. Rate of Adoption with Adjusted Resister Modifier

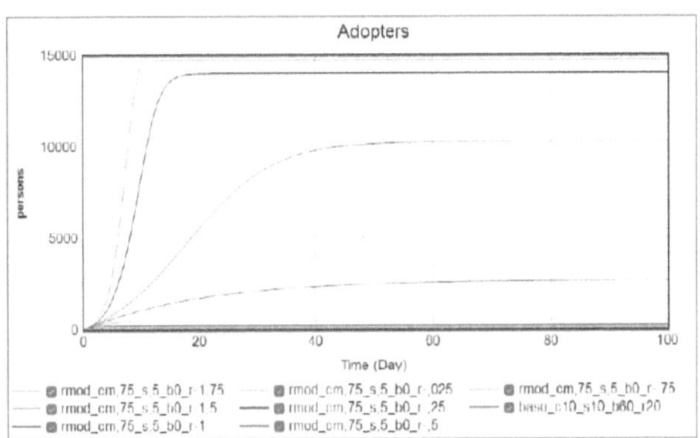

Figure 11. Total Adopters (out of 16,000) with Adjusted Resister Modifier

# COMING DOWN

A warm front had come in, a few inches of slow followed by hours of freezing rain. Early this year. The slush flowed along the gutters and plugged up the storm drain, and small lakes of ice water threatened to consume the streets and walkways. Cyd considered the four-story brownstone that loomed across the street. He took a drag from his cigarette, shielding it from the rain with his other hand, and he hesitated. He had to be careful. Sneaking into an apartment was harder than it sounded, especially as a middle-aged male who looked as disheveled as he had become. He couldn't wait in the foyer; someone would see him coming and get suspicious when he tried to come in behind them. There was a clear line of sight through the glass windows to the street, and anyone could see that he wasn't actually waiting for a friend to buzz him in.

So he sat across the street on the corner near a small café. Smoking a cigarette and pretending to check his email on his phone. The chance came as he saw a familiar pair of men round the corner and head toward the apartment building. Cyd had decided these were the ones. They were men, so they were less likely to feel threatened by him or suspicious. Men were more often oblivious to the dangers of the world, rarely having to face them. Furthermore, there were two of them, roommates, or just friends, talking loudly and laughing. They wouldn't notice or care, hopefully. Cyd tossed his cigarette in the gutter, picked up the sealed bag of cold fast food he carried, and sped up across the street, timing his walk to come in behind them.

He followed them in with no eye contact and a low "thanks, bro" before pausing in the first-floor hallway, pretending to check his phone again.

The taller one turned. "You looking for someone?"

"Travers?" Cyd replied, gesturing to the bag of fast food in his hand. "Delivery."

The shorter one smiled. "Oh, yeah, that's me." As he motioned to hand over the bag."

Cyd paused. "What's the first name?"

"Ah, you got me." He raised his hands lightly and played it off as a joke before turning back down the hallway to catch up with his roommate.

Cyd headed slowly up the stairs. He knew from her more unhinged blog posts that she was on the top floor facing the construction site, which would put her on the left side of the hallway. He had to talk to her. She knew more than anyone, and she was decaying like he was. Who knows how much time she had. She hadn't posted anything for a while now. It was uncharacteristic. The vinyl treads of the stairway cracked and creaked below his feet. The wooden banisters had a dirty and polished look. Thousands of hands had rubbed them smooth and caked in a greasy epoxy of dead skin cells and carpet dust.

Each step flexed and creaked, sending echoes through the stairwell. There was no stealth here, just deception. Second floor, keep moving. Third floor, 'I shouldn't be this out of breath. When did I eat last? Tuesday? What day is it?'

He finally reached the fourth floor and peered down the hallway to the fire escape at its end. Only three doors on the left. Odds could be worse. He tried to move slowly but deliberately enough to not arouse suspicion.

It wasn't door one. He heard a yell from inside, a teenager arguing with her parents? The second door was quieter. He knocked on the door. No answer. He knocked again. "Fuck, what if she's not home." He couldn't pull this stunt over and over. But wait, a noise on the far side, someone approaching.

Footsteps, a shadow, creeping through the doorframe at his feet. Metal-on-metal scraping of a deadbolt. The faint jingle of a chain. When it opened, the light blinded him as it streamed in through the window behind the man who now stood in front of him.

"Yeah?" The man asked through a greying beard that looked too old for his face. "What's up?" It was the wrong door. Stacey was single. She mentioned it several times. But maybe not, maybe a fling, maybe a relative, who knows? God, why did Cyd always do this? Was he a bad person? Making benign but stupid assumptions about women. Jesus, it shouldn't be so automatic, right? Like the therapist all over again. Maybe he was just a chauvinist. He was trying though. Was it better that he was so painfully aware of it?

"Can I help you? What do you want?" The man was impatient; how long had Cyd been staring at him? The hinges creaked as he gave up and moved to shut it.

"Sorry," Cyd blurted out. "Zoning out, I've been making deliveries all night. Is Stacey Travers here?

"No, she's next door. Don't you have the apartment number?"

"Yeah, sorry. Like I said, been up all night. Have a good one." The man shut the door, closing him off to the natural world once again and trapping him in the dingy, dated air of the hall. But he had done it; he knew where she lived. A shadow passed across the peephole in the door. Fuck! The guy was looking at him standing there. Shuffle to the side before he calls the cops. God, he must look like a serial killer right now. Good thing he was in Massachusetts; the guy is less likely to have a gun, ergo, less likely to shoot him through the door.

But he moved slowly, so focused on finding her he didn't know what he would say.

What if she thought he was crazy, and had been making all of this up to sell books or something? Was he just a deranged stalker?

Worse, what if she was the crazy one and had lost it completely. What if she attacked him when he mentioned his visions?

What if he found her hanging from the ceiling fan? Maybe she thought about it as much as he did. Do ceiling fans even support that kind of weight? Where had he gotten that idea anyway? It feels like a movie cliché, but he couldn't think of a single example.

It didn't matter. He had come this far.

He listened to the door and heard nothing from the inside but the raspy whir of an old air conditioner.

He knocked; it gave way. The lock!

It was open; it hadn't latched when she opened it last.

He wouldn't have to break in, but if she was home, it would be more suspicious. Best pretend not to notice and knock again.

And again.

A little harder.

A little louder.

Nothing.

The static whir of the air conditioner, it clicked and turned off.

He pushed the door slightly. "Hello?" He called into the room through the opening. "Ms. Travers? Stacey?"

Still nothing.

What if she wasn't home.

What if she came back while he was in there.

*Go down, son. Submit.*

Not again, not now.

Fuck no.

He had come this far; he was committed.

He tapped the door a little more until it sounded a sharp crack through the halls like an alarm bell. Still no response. "Stacey?" He called again. "I'm not a creep. I'm here because I need your help, and I think you need mine." No response. The air conditioner clicked on again, and he heard the distant, muffled shouting of the family down the hall. Something, something "tired of this" something. But nothing from Stacey's. "I hear him, too. He calls out to me and wants me to come to him… it's getting worse. I… I think he killed my wife."

He opened the door all the way and stepped into the dusty hallway of the apartment. He misjudged the weight and forced it too fast, shuddering at the noise of the doorstop spring on the hallway wall, matching its vibrations. No blinding flash of light; she had dark curtains drawn on the other side of the living room, letting in only small blades of pale light to pierce through, seeming solely to darken the shadows. Cyd closed the door behind him. "I came in. I want to talk. I need to talk to you. I have no one else. There is something happening."

No fearful rustling of a terrified victim hiding in closets. No metallic scraping of a kitchen knife being unsheathed, ready to slash. No presence. The apartment was empty. What should he do? She wasn't home.

*Escape. Escape and submit!*

Cyd moved to the living room and sat on the worn couch, stirring a cloud of dust particles to swirl chaotically in the intruding beams of sunlight. The room was filthy. Books strewn around the floor, some randomly, others stacked neatly before being knocked over and cascading along the polished hardwood like so many New England apartments. Books on the occult, monsters, biology, zoology, cognitive psychology. Some were marked with small yellow post-its, some open with notes scribbled in margins. Some stacks were just pages torn from the books with messages and terrifying scribble of the teeth and long, clawed body that he knew so well. They chittered through his dreams and murdered. His spine felt cold.

What now? All he could do was wait. He wouldn't get another chance. He spied a small stack of notebooks below the coffee table. Labeled by date. He pulled the most recent and flipped through the pages.

∞ ∞ ∞

October 2nd

Officially fired today. They said I'd become a "professional liability" because of what I've been writing. Of course. I guess it was bound to happen sooner or later after they stopped publishing me. I just wish Aaron had the balls to say it to me himself. Going to meet with MacArthur tomorrow.

Questions:

- Remember me?

- Account of what happened.

- How are his nightmares holding up? Swamp or wetland in dreams? Any animals? Pale white?

- The voice. Ask him to describe it, what does it say to him. (Don't describe it yourself. Don't put an idea in his head that he can anchor on. Need clear, untainted description.)

- Is it getting more urgent? Is it getting faster? Is it getting more common?

- Anyone else I should talk to? Who else knows? Any family?

- Has he been to the art gallery? Gertie Bellefour? ~~Sean Travers?~~

October 3rd

Fucked that up. Mac was quiet and suspicious and polite at first, but I think he knew he recognized me. I told him about my dreams. He didn't like it. Tension throughout his body. I know he recognized them. He wouldn't admit it. But he didn't tell me to leave. Didn't want to give contact info. Said, "I just want to keep it out of my life." Not sure what he meant by "it." I think he wanted it to mean the stress/story. But "it" meant the thing, the thing that speaks.

I followed him home. Fucking noticed me about three-quarters of the way. I think. But he took a circuitous route and snuck into the back door of his tiny single-family cottage in lower Cambridge.

I saw the curtain shift. He was either looking for followers or expecting me to follow him all the way. I think he was looking for me. I stayed behind the corner for a few minutes. I don't know when I left, but the sun was going down. Nothing stirred in the house. But I heard a door slam, echoing through the quiet street just above the distant murmur of traffic. It was right as I walked away, but I couldn't turn back to inspect. Something felt wrong about it. So, I tucked my tail. I'm going to try again in a few days.

October 5th

go down, go down. Always fucking down. Why? Physically? Emotionally? what the fuck does it have to do with that fucking corpse? Yes, it was horrible; yes, I see it whenever I close my eyes. Yes, I hear the screams. Not a memory, at least not one that I've had. It's real. They aren't my screams; they were his. Hundreds of books on PTSD and haven't found anything quite like this. How can I hear screams I haven't heard? Sean? How the hell did I know they were Seans? They weren't mine. I know his voice, but I knew them to be Sean's, as if he's deliberately taunting me. Like in a dream, when you know the house is yours even though it's set up like your mom's. Is he doing this on purpose? Is it telepathy or something simpler?

It's worse than a headache. I have to hold my skull together and try to vomit in the toilet. Like my brain is trying to escape. The terror, all the time. It's creeping higher and higher. Reaching for a pinnacle that it doesn't achieve. What will cave first? My body or my mind? Going to go drink until I pass out.

October 6th

Hurts too much, can't write. Feel like I've been poisoned. Found oxy and coke on my dresser. Don't remember getting it. I must have called Brittany last night. Hope we didn't hook up, but knowing her, it's likely. I didn't notice any missing cash. Just another fuck up to add to the growing list of fuck ups. Why am I so worthless? Maybe I'm better off dead instead of taking up space in this apartment. I'm sure it could make someone happy. I need sunlight. The vibrations of last night still throb like a 90s industrial band. Maybe the headache is just withdrawal from a moment of peace.

Sweaty, disgusting peace. I can't stop thinking of the drill.
Opening a window and letting out all the evil in my head,
trying so desperately to crack me open and escape.


October 7<sup>th</sup>
Almost feel human again… going for a walk while
there are still leaves to gawk at.


On a bench, surrounded by assholes. 07 October.


I don't feel the spill.
I used to be unburdened
when I wrote, it was survival.
A slow release of pressure, to prevent a rupture.
Avoiding the coming burst
blowing flesh and brain against
walls and floors, and ceiling fans.
And teeth! Teeth and bits of
sharpened skull making indents
in the drywall.


Am I healthy yet?
The unspoken cost of health must be to
Lose the beautiful darkness.
Those monsters, lying in wait
writing prose, not pretty.
I feel no lighter and
thriving may not be better
than surviving.
I don't even care if these stanzas match.

October 12<sup>th</sup>

Fuck, it's 5pm and I forgot I was going to check on MacArthur. It's been a while now. I think I'm good. I think I'm good. Going to head over at 10. The sun sets so late here.


October 13<sup>th</sup>

FIRST DRAFT:: A full account of my evening with Mac, 12 October.

The weather was cool. The hidden chill of a humid night as summer retreats into autumn. The October wind has been warming for years, but tonight, it cut a chill through my jacket, freezing the bead of sweat I had accumulated on my forehead on the brisk walk to my objective. Shadows crept along the streets, stalking through the alleyways and reclaiming the city for their own, if only for a fleeting time in anticipation of the coming winter. Yet the dark remains ever threatening; the streetlights creak under the oppression of horrible black, poised on the periphery. Light feels heavy and travels less far, ~~reminding us that~~ we are all only a few steps away from the horrors that lurk just beyond its tired gaze.

The sidewalks are cracked and broken; they'd be indistinguishable from the pulverized asphalt if they didn't hover just a few inches from the surface. The curbs are less ~~of~~ a reassuring boundary ~~and more of~~ than a subtle trap, reminding me that a wrong step can lead to pain and suffering ~~in the ditch~~. Mac's house sat on the east side of the city, neighborhoods in the grips of the heroin crisis but hidden under the glamourous shade of the Ivy League universities just a mile to the west. Mac kept up with his own maintenance. He was a long-standing pillar of the neighborhood while the properties to his left and right rotted away. The house glowed white with new siding wrapped halfway around the exterior. But he must have run out of money; the left exterior wall was still exposed, and the wood was peeling. The first-floor windows didn't quite match the aesthetic; slightly beige but new and recently installed. The second floor still had the original windows of the property as it was built in the 1930s. But through the second-floor window, I could see the torn debris and sharp edges of fresh windows leaning against a wall, waiting to be installed. He must have been doing it himself, one at a time. Explains the window color, which looks like a "cheapest option at the home improvement store" situation. I couldn't blame him though. In the New England winter, heating costs rise every year. He probably still heats with oil.

Approaching the house, I glanced along the street. It wasn't late yet. In Kendall Square and across the river, newly arrived college students are in full force, wandering around and causing a ruckus. But not here. There is nothing here. Those who pass through are lost, and even ~~those are less common now~~ the lost dwindle now. ~~A product of the rideshare generation likely.~~ About this time, I noticed a faint humming. Sometimes, my ears act up, and I'm used to my heart rate elevating for no reason. But it was more, I watched the moths circle around a nearby streetlight in ~~chaotic and beautiful fashion~~ chaos and beauty when I heard a familiar clicking, sharp and cavernous in the darkness. The scuttling of looming terrors shuffling through my brain. It's a shade, nothing more. ~~The voice compels me to~~ I look east, and ~~I~~ see a shadow of a shadow. The faintest outline of a spider, not much larger. Larger than a man. A vision of pale black against the dark. Just looming beyond the veil.

*Go down.* It said to me. *Follow.* It beckoned. But I turned my attention back to the house. Perhaps the terror came for me; perhaps it protected Mac. ~~But there was no way to tell.~~ The looming migraine began to grow, pulsing through my brow and jaw. I only had a few more minutes. ~~Migraines follow whenever I defy the terror.~~ Whenever I force myself to focus on other things, it gets harder and harder. I have only a few minutes before my vision starts to blur from the pain.

I crossed the narrow, crumbling street and through his ~~broken~~ crooked fence. The stained curtains whispered through the windows like spirits spying through the other side. ~~At once, as though a hidden draft permeated the house.~~ I stepped softly up the concrete stairway to his front porch. ~~I wore~~ my running shoes ~~to pad~~ padded my footsteps. Look again for passersbys. No one. Nobody ~~here~~ cared. The city has forgotten their squalor. Quietly waiting for the inconvenient ~~residents~~ to die ~~off~~ so they can gentrify the neighborhood. I listened through the door. Nothing. Minutes go by. Still nothing.

~~There was~~ A faint green light ~~coming from~~ in the right window. ~~Changing randomly~~ from green, to blue, to grey. ~~A television.~~ I ~~slowly stepped away from the door and over to the window to peer in.~~ shuffled along the wall. Rounding the edge, I strained to make out the dim shapes on the other side. Movement, or was that a trick of the light? I couldn't see the source. It reflected off outdated floral wallpaper from the back room and silhouetted the vague shapes of what I assumed were the covered furniture of an old sitting room, lying untouched for who knows how long.

But the ~~darkness obscured my vision and~~ void was thick and overbearing. I tried to make sense of a blurry mass in the doorway. Pop! The streetlight behind me burst with ~~the briefest~~ a flash of light before plunging the rest of the street into darkness. ~~Before my world went back, the flashing bulb illuminated the mass.~~ In that flash, I saw Mac nearly pressed up against the other side of the glass. Only a few inches from me. ~~his eyes glinting with fiery tears. He had a frantic look~~ One eye wide and frantic, he looked terrified, relieved, and furious. How long had he been staring at me through the window? Who was he expecting? His wrinkled ~~collared~~ shirt was untucked on one side, covering the ~~unmistakable~~ bulge of a pistol shoved hastily into his pocket. In his right hand, a long chef's knife flashed in the light. Fuck! How long was he staring at me ~~before I realized it was him~~?

His face was ragged and aged. Thinned out from dehydration. His skin glistened in crusty salt lines of a man waking in a cold sweat and refusing to shower. This wasn't the ~~polite, composed~~ man I met ~~a few~~ weeks ago, sitting quietly on the park bench with his tacklebox as police dragged a mutilated corpse up onto the riverbanks. His face contorted in the wild look of a prey animal. My last glimpse of those eyes as they met my gaze and betrayed a hint of recognition. I saw the heave of his chest and faint curl to his lip. I think ~~a part of him~~ he was relieved it was me.

When the light went out, the universe turned black. I think the power may have gone out. There was no TV, only the heavy thudding of footsteps shaking the old house. ~~moving quickly and deliberately through the house. A crash from inside tells me that he must have tripped over something.~~ A crash on the inside; I think he tripped. I backed away from the window ~~quickly~~ and turned to run but forgot about the concrete steps. ~~I heard the pop in my left leg as I tumbled down to the concrete walkway below.~~ I caught the edge of my foot and tumbled, feeling the pop when I caught my weight on my left leg. I don't think it's broken; I could limp on it, ~~after that point. Probably a sprain.~~ wiping the tears with my sleeve.

The walking stopped. He wasn't coming to kill me. The lights of the house flickered on, and I heard his desperate and exasperated shriek. The catharsis of pain and suffering. He was hurt; he suddenly had a visible injury into which he would pour all his pent-up suffering. He screamed again. I heard his voice break and crack as he broke into sobs. ~~I wanted to run.~~ My skin burned, and my muscles twitched, all screaming at me to run. I wanted to leave so much. I felt the darkness closing around his small house but ~~couldn't do it~~ stayed rooted to the ground.

*Submit!* The horrible voice crept into my bones. It wanted me to leave. Was it talking to me or Mac? *Submit!*

I couldn't. ~~If he was hurt, it was my fault.~~ I had to ~~at least~~ call 911. I reached for my phone but had lost it. Likely dropped in the bushes somewhere during my fall. I steadied myself and groped around for the stairs.

Working my way to a stand and testing my weight on my ankle. Shooting pain, but the bones seemed intact. I hobbled my way back to the porch and to the front door. The howling shook the walls and cracked stone, but suddenly it stopped. ~~The shrieking stopped, but~~ I could hear his lonely gasps and whimpering on the other side.

I tried to call out. "Mac? Are you okay?" but I felt the words leak from my mouth without force, without intention. Rhetorical in response to the weak, shaken mutters of the terrified. ~~Fear had robbed me of a voice. I gripped the icy doorknob, and it gave way with regrettable ease.~~ I fumbled for the doorknob and found it unlocked. The door creaked open, and I heard his gasps echo through the house.

"Mr. MacArthur?" I ~~croaked, barely above a whisper.~~ called. "It's okay. It's Stacey… it's… it's not them."

~~No response, just~~ Answered only by the raspy, tortured breathing of a man losing hope; I limped into the ~~room~~ foyer and felt a chill come from ~~the door~~ behind ~~me. Glancing into~~ In the street, I saw the haunting mass just beyond recognition, not moving, just watching. A light grew as an old car rounded the nearby corner and continued down the street toward the highway on-ramp. The light passed through the vision of the beckoning creature to reveal nothing. So lurking mass beyond sight, waiting to pounce. Just the thin brick walls of the opposite building, marred in the fingerpaint of unskilled graffiti. ~~Just another reminder that my sanity is gone. Had I caused all of this? Was I schizophrenic now?~~ Did I misinterpret ~~my~~ our conversation ~~with Mac and simply~~

~~break into the home of an unsuspecting senior, causing a heart attack? Christ, did I just kill someone?~~

I ~~frantically~~ reached out ahead of me, trying to find the source of the now low moans of my dying victim. ~~I had to do something. But~~ I couldn't tell which room he was in. The faint, glow~~ing light~~ of the television ~~had come back on~~ covered the room in a pond-scum green. The same glow revealed an older, uncovered couch in the next room. Dark stains on the doorknob and along the floor sliding into the living room. ~~God, I hoped it wasn't blood.~~

"Mac? Do you need help?"

A creak in the next room. ~~"Yes," I heard him croak.~~ A malicious croak, a desperate gurgle.

I entered the living room, feeling ~~the~~ warm, dark stains and smelling the metallic waft of the blood on my hands. The coating turned thick and sticky as it penetrated the creases in my palms and knuckles.

Mac was lying on the floor, propped up against the side of a loveseat and staring at me. ~~His eyes wide in an unearthly gaze that looked through me to the outside world.~~ One eye was wide and wild. It remained fixed on me. The other drooped and stared through me to the outside world. The glinting of his kitchen knife dulled by blood leaking from his ribcage. I ~~tried to discern his injury from the doorway.~~ crept along the floor toward his silhouette, crouching at his side to ~~look at his~~ assess the wound. His eyes were pale white, and his mind ~~seemed like it~~ was trapped in another world. He reached for my shoulder.

"Don't... go... down... there." He croaked. ~~Struggling for air~~ through ~~short,~~ shallow breaths. "There's nothing but death." He sputtered, and his dark blood stained his chin and shirt.

"Down where?" I think I asked. "Where is he?"

"Not he. ~~It's~~ not a he." Mac tried to string his thoughts together. "It preys. It…. consumes. It can't come for me, but you did."

~~I think~~ I apologized. ~~But I can't remember.~~ The weight of fear lifted, leaving space for sorrow and regret. I wanted to take him to a hospital and leaned in to check his breathing. ~~When it happened, I was almost too slow to react.~~

In an instant, the pale fog lifted from his eyes, and he gazed at me in full recognition and rage. "No!" He ~~shouted as he~~ reached for the handle and pulled the kitchen knife from his chest, swinging wildly at me. ~~Swinging wildly at me, he stared at my eyes and aimed at my neck.~~ I ~~was able to roll~~ rolled onto my side and dodged the worst of it. ~~managing only a small cut in my face. I rolled away and tried to stand, covering my chin to stop the bleeding.~~ He cut my face, and I tried to stand. ~~I hit him in the face with my right hand, not to hurt him, just a reflex from past horrors.~~ Mac screamed wildly like an animal and tried to crawl toward me, revealing ~~the extent of~~ the pool of blood he had lost already, creeping across the parquet. I pulled myself away, but he lost energy, and his voice faded. The clouds of his eyes rolled back in, and he tried to speak again. "Please, let there be something ~~after~~ beyond this." He sobbed and coughed and vomited blood onto the floor. With his lung clear for only an instant, he gasped. "Underground. Old T. They'll eat us all."

He dropped his shaking hand from his chest wound and looked me in the eye. ~~Before I could understand his intention,~~ he held the kitchen knife to his neck and dragged it across his throat. He kept ~~looking at me, staring into my soul.~~ his eyes on me, and I watched them bulge and recede, the intense, pitiful stare transformed into a doll's disinterested gaze. Those pupils, so wide. The whites ~~were so bright until they~~ brightened and faded. The blood started slowly but burst forth as he found his jugular. He never stopped staring at me even as his body shivered and he slumped to the side, pausing ~~briefly in one final act of defiance~~ before he slid off ~~the side of~~ the loveseat and fell to the floor. ~~As~~ Mac's ~~slumped to the side, and his throat opened when his head pressed against the floor in opposition to his torso.~~ head hit the floor, bending backward and opening like floodgates. His body stopped shaking, his lungs stopped heaving, and he was gone. I ~~hoped to see a look of~~ saw no peace on his face, ~~but saw~~ only terror, missing teeth, and the silent ~~pools of~~ blood ~~forming under his mouth and nostrils~~ spreading across the floor, trying to swallow the room. ~~All I could think of in that moment, was about what similar fate might be waiting for me.~~

October 14th
Still haven't been charged. Maybe a person of interest? Likely still a person of interest. ~~Since I've done journalism work before and I showed up at his house late at night.~~ I'll probably be charged with something. I don't know

how reckless endangerment works. Third-degree manslaughter? ~~I don't know.~~ I thought about looking it up, but I don't care. Mac had ~~a bunch of~~ a few illegal guns in his house and 103 tabs of ecstasy. Only his fingerprints were on the knife, and it was a clear suicide, and I called the police. All that, coupled with a few recent complaints from his neighbors about the "crazy old man" screaming at night, worked in my favor.

October 16th

I have to find the end. My brain won't stop swelling in my skull. I need to vent it. I have to get it out. The drill calls out stronger each day.  Just a small bit, right above the ear. Just enough to get the fluid out.

I just need a sharp enough bit. Something to make it fast. What did Mac see?  I don't know of any abandoned MBTA lines. But there has to be something. I can't go on living like this. Fine, you fucking bastard, I'm coming.

# THE MESSENGER

In the dark. In the cold, hard, and slimy places underground, the messenger had taken over. It was hatched like all the others into a treacherous existence of hunger and misery. Its kin chirped and searched and fed and searched through the darkness. Hunger, always hunger. A never-ending tedium of existence, of survival. But not the messenger; the messenger was weak. It was frail; its legs were smaller; its hide was softer. It could not search and search without end. Weakness begat weakness, and it waivered and withered. He would surely starve to death, like so many others. Too small even to attract the voracious eyes of the hunters, who merely stepped over him, a minor irritation on their way to find prey. So small, unworthy of consumption.

The messenger was hatched like all the others. Its frail body lurched along the tunnels and sucked on the marrows and squirmy things that coated the festering remains of prey.

But the messenger was different. He wasn't like the others who lived in silence, caring not for the agonies or ecstasies that life could offer. They mindlessly searched and fed like pistons in some bloodthirsty contraption.

They felt nothing, but the messenger felt pain. Pain all around it, echoing through the chambers, rattling tiny pebbles shaken loose from the pits. Pain that twisted the world and warped the darkness. This was not the messenger's pain; it didn't emanate from its body, but invaded its mind from the outside. It left imprints on the dark surroundings when the hunters hauled in living food. Not his pain, the other's pain. The food's pain. The fresh, live food that the hunters dragged into their home piled up on the mound. Sometimes, it screamed and writhed in futile resistance. The messenger was hatched like all the others, but it felt their screams and knew their fear. Fear had no meaning to the monster beyond the calling card of something fresh, and something tasty. Food screamed quietly from afar but got louder. Loud was good, and it meant soon, the hunters would drag the shivering corpse into the den and leave more scraps for the harvesters and, eventually, for the messenger. Loud was good. Loud screams meant food.

The messenger was hatched like all the others, but it soon gathered the strength to drag itself to the pits when it heard food screaming through the air. He heard the screaming food before the others. Sometimes, he arrived first. He got more food when he beat the harvesters to the pit. He waited until the hunters picked the biggest parts of the carcass and leaped into the high places to eat in peace. The messenger feasted on the fresh meat until the harvesters arrived and poked and jabbed him aside to feast for themselves.

Food sent signals that only the messenger could feel. Food wafted in misery near and far, floating through the dark places in the world. The messenger was hatched like all the others, but soon, he felt his power grow along with his body. He got more meat little by little. He learned to vibrate with excitement when food was near. His vibrations traveled into the dark places, and food began to feel them. The messenger began to vibrate signals through the void, and food would change. Food became aware. Food began to vibrate back. Sometimes, it would shudder, and bristle, and run away. Sometimes, it would pause and carry on. Sometimes, food would wander closer, wading through the vibrations to find the source. It would try to investigate. Food heard his voice through the void and felt the resonance as it returned to him. Food shuddered in fear, but food began to crawl.

The messenger was hatched like all the others, but it couldn't see like the hunters or move like the harvesters. It stayed still and waited. It grew clever and ate more to survive. It grew fat and soft until its legs couldn't support its weight. It lurched and dragged its round body forward along the tunnel floors until it felt food beneath its hulking mass of soft flesh. It fed on the remnants. The sloppy remains of what the hunters left behind and the harvesters couldn't find. But each find made the messenger stronger. It could vibrate harder and see further. The messenger pushed further and started to discern visions in the dark. It heard strange noises. Living things, warm food. And it hungered more with each meal. It began to discern shapes, sizes, thoughts, feelings. It knew when food was happy, scared, or angry.

The messenger was hatched like all the others, but as it grew fat, the others began to notice him. When they couldn't find food, they would surround him, moving in closer and beginning to poke and prod, looking for loose limbs and easy morsels. When food was scarce, he was a morsel. The harvesters came for him; they were desperate and dangerous. They took pieces and left, and his anger grew. Until he vibrated into their minds. He recognized when they would come for him. He pulsed, lashing out in an explosion of fear and rage. He reached into their minds and kept them away. They wanted food. He gave them to each other. They turned on the weakest and sated their hunger. After the fray, the messenger slumped along the floor to feed on the scraps. He was more alert, more mindful. He pulsed harder and saw farther, spewing darkness upon darkness and laying traps for his prey.

The messenger was hatched like all the others. But it no longer feared. The hunters roamed and killed and feasted, but he saw their minds and fed them others. He readied the weak ones whenever food was scarce. He provided for the others. He reached out farther and farther and grew comfortable with his prey. He changed the messages he sent. Sometimes, food did fear his pulse. The warping paused; the raspy breaths of hairy things slowed and began to wander. Food liked comfort, not fear. And when the messenger made it comfortable, food sought out the messenger. Creepy, crawling, wretched things crept through the dirt to their doom. With each meal, its power grew.

Through the pits and walls, mud-slick, hairy food lurched forward to the messenger. When harvesters took notice, they intercepted the prey and took what they could. But the messenger kept them at bay. First, they left scraps, then they waited patiently as the messenger ate its fill. The messenger provided and set them on the insolent. The rest fell in line. The messenger delivered. The scraps of the hunters were insufficient. The messenger could lure larger food that barked, whinnied, and snarled. It honked and brayed and squawked and screamed and whimpered and cried. And the sound became pleasure.

Then the messenger felt the curious prey, out alone in the void. It was subtle and violent. When he vibrated too much, some died. Other times, they lashed out at other prey, and the other prey would separate or kill each other before they could seek the messenger. The messenger was hatched like all the others, but now it hunted for sport. It grew complex and curious. It vibrated every way it could, repeating what resonated most. *Grag ghlogh ftann goe dogn flagh no fltagn.* Food shuddered when it spoke. *Gggoooo doffghn. Doowwwnn. Go down.* Food became curious, and it wandered. It sensed when it was close and submitted itself to his home. It came to the pit willingly. It loved him, and it sacrificed itself on his altar.

Finally, humans sought out the messenger. It touched their dreams and made them curious. Seeking relief. Seeking release. The messenger learned their minds and groped their psyches for the broken fragments of their souls. The more the messenger reached out, the more submitted themselves to the pit. Food was scarce for the hunters. They returned with small things and left none to share. While the hunters were out, the harvesters feasted on fresh meat, always feeding the messenger. The harvesters grew strong, and the hunters grew weak. The harvesters expanded the pits of pits of black muck and poison. Food came to the messenger, and they protected him.

The messenger was king. The messenger was God. The harvesters ate their share before leaving the rest to him. The hunters withered and couldn't chase their prey. They stayed in the pits, sneaking scraps and sucking marrow. They withered and turned on each other. They hated the messenger, if hate was possible for such a thing. But the messenger provided. The messenger was hatched like all the others, but now it was king. Now, it was God.

But the messenger needed more. Food was less and less. They consumed all, and the abyss grew dark and devoid. The colony needed more. When he reached out, food was too far away to find him. He reached out far but only lapped on the doors of their minds like the rising tide on a rocky shore. It began to hunger, and it feared its colony. When it heard the familiar strings of a broken psyche vibrating against the abyss. It was the same, but it was different. Its mind echoed with fresh thoughts of prey and plenty like a spring breeze in the dark tunnels. It knew where food was. The messenger was hatched like all the others, but somehow, it had learned to speak. *More. It's not enough. Show me more. Not crazy at all. Come to me and submit. You belong here. You belong to me. You belong to us.*

∞ ∞ ∞

Adrian couldn't stop crying, and she didn't know why. Ninth grade, sitting cross-legged across from another awkward teen on the old gym mats on the basketball court. Golden sunlight filled the room, reflecting off the polished floor, scorching eyes and painting the cinderblock walls dedicated to school spirit. 'Go Spartans! Fight!' It made the room warm and almost made her forget why they were there as her eyelids slowly descended and her mind drifted off.

Across from her sat the other girl. LaShauna something. Adrian knew her from the school bus. She lived in the patch behind Cumby's on 3$^{rd}$ Ave. Her curly hair always bounced rhythmically while she trotted away from home to the bus stop. Adrian liked it; the bouncing almost covered up her shame and terror and kept attention away from her thick makeup, covering bruises and cuts. Adrian couldn't remember the last name. She usually forgot names right after introducing herself in some show of either arrogance or self-consciousness. Every time she had to meet someone new, she was so worried about messing it up that she inevitably did. Adrian and the mystery girl were paired up, staring at each other, sitting on the blue wrestling mats, much to Coach Stevenson's dismay as he scowled across the room, snapping at people to take their shoes off lest they ruin the foam. The mats were spread haphazardly across the floor. A hundred other pairs sat around them in a mixture of thick silence and stifled giggles. "Take this seriously," Mr. Johnson told them before they started. "You might learn something unexpected about yourself."

There was a mental health crisis at school. Adam Beckenridge tried to kill himself over the weekend. He was the third this month. His kid sister (seven, I think) found him in the bathtub with his wrist cut. He never lifted the drain plug and sat for nearly an hour in a pool of his own blood. They heard he lived, but no one could confirm it. He wasn't answering his cell phone and hadn't been back to school. Three girls hospitalized for anorexia this semester, not to mention four kids found crying in the bathrooms by teachers in the past three weeks. The school thought it had something to do with isolation and loneliness.

The plus side was: no classes today. But instead, Adrian got to ogle a stranger she didn't really know. A mental health day. It was supposed to build empathy. They started with something more active. They called it a privilege walk, one of those exercises where everyone lines up along a wall and plays Simon Says to see whose life is easiest. Adrian always ended up toward the back. But it was mostly because she was poor.

After a few more group therapy sessions, they were primed for the final exercise. "The eyes are the window to the soul if you believe that sort of thing." Mr. Johnson began. "If not, you'll see where that comes from with this exercise. It's simple. All you are going to do is pair up with someone you don't know and make eye contact for a full minute without talking." He paused until the nervous shifting and laughter died down. "On the social science side, this has been shown to increase empathy. But on the more human side, we are so wrapped up in the trappings and structures of human interactions that we are never able to truly connect. You might find that you learn more about your partner, or even yourself, in this one minute than you know about your closest friends."

More shifting and giggles, but the laughing felt forced. The teenagers searched frantically for someone they liked to alleviate their stress. But Mr. Johnson had been around long enough to know who was friends with whom. After splitting everyone up into pairs, he did another pass to ensure no one was with someone who would make it easy on them. Adrian was paired with whatshername and quickly tried to establish some common ground. Each smiled nervously, and they tried to think of an icebreaker, but nothing came to mind, and they waited in silence, each shifting their weight back and forth. "Once everyone is quiet, we'll begin." Mr. Johnson's voice echoed from the other side of the gym, where he finished his second pass. Thinking so much about the horror of eye contact made Adrian deliberately avoid it. She stared at Mr. Johnson like a hawk and a mouse. She gawked intently at the basketball hoops and inspected the quality of the paint on the back wall. 'Go Spartans! Fight!' All the while, she felt the pressure of the impending ordeal build and build.

"Time starts… now." Adrian met LaShauna, the stranger's gaze, and shared a nervous smile. She tried to make it happen, to take it seriously. She stared at a mole between her eyebrows but began to worry it would make her self-conscious. She only saw the stranger's face for a moment. She saw her smile relax, not frowning, just neutral, and felt her own do the same. Adrian saw the micro-creases in her face expand and expose her mind. She saw pain, loneliness, anger, joy, stress, and she felt all of those as if they were her own emotions. But she supposed they were, and she felt the burrow deep. The stranger knew her pain as well, but her eyes showed no judgment. Adrian felt the pit rise in her stomach and her face heat up as her tear glands burst forth in a torrent of emotion that escaped her body as a tear, slowly grinding its way down her face. Then another.

Then another.

The stranger's brow furrowed, and her eyes softened with concern but remained fixed. Adrian saw the shadow in her. And as her eyes welled up, she held it back enough to ensure Adrian was crying alone. And she did, with hushed breaths and shudders, hoping desperately that her nose didn't run. Why was she crying? The trappings of a social shield stripped so unceremoniously away. Was anyone else crying? Was she alone?

"Fifteen seconds." She heard Mr. Johnson's faint voice echo from across a canyon.

"Christ, is that fifteen seconds in or fifteen seconds left?" She thought, wishing this moment would end, but unable to stop. Sobbing quietly, feeling exposed, fraudulent, and hopeless. She was standing naked in the swamps, fearing hungry beasts. She wallowed back into her own mind, almost forgetting about the other girl's when she saw it emerge.

There was something else. Hidden in the stranger's eyes, in the black pools behind the decaying shield from pain. For a moment, Adrian saw the corporeal form of the other girl fade away, leaving only pallid eyes staring back at her. Was she even there? Or was Adrian seeing her own eyes, her own soul. Behind that shield of black nothing lies something deeper and darker than nothing. A presence that hid beneath her skin, burrowing into her skull. A black tree that grew like a creeping moss, filling the folds of her brain and laying deep roots along her spine and into her heart. Her lungs filled with dirt, and her chest halted. From the cracks in her psyche, light and dark burst out into the void and created life.

Adrian blinked, and the tree was gone. She stared at the woman before her, mid-thirties, skinny and dead. Well, not yet. She heaved and gargled and coughed as blood and vomit poured from the open wound in her throat. Her eyes rolled back, and her skull followed. A horrible shriek, a piercing banshee cry. Adrian heard it but could not see the source; perhaps it was herself. But it echoed into nothing as the gash in the woman's throat split and spread as if severed with an invisible blade.

She saw the spinal cord exposed as the jugulars ripped and tendons snapped. A pale, soft cord of tissue along the spine. She watched it split and tear and heard the vertebrae crunch the cartilage and crack as they slammed into each other. Blood poured down her neck, desperately searching for her brain, finding her chest and the floor. Her head came undone but never fell. And as the poor woman's suffering should have ended, she fell into a shuddering seizure of death knells as her chest shot upward into the air. She hung as if suspended by a string, motionless and eternal.

Adrian no longer heard the screams but felt them. The woman's chest split along the center of the ribcage, peeling back the bones like a duffel bag and letting her heart and lungs, normally anchored at the neck, slip through and dangle at the knees. The horrible wrenching continued, and Adrian felt the pain as if it were her own body.

"Fuck, it's me," she thought. "This is how I die, I'm going to die, I'm going to die, I'm dying, I'm dying." Her lungs collapsed, and she coughed a thick mixture of blood and vomit onto the hanging meat.

"And TIME." Mr. Johnson's voice was close. Adrian was cross-legged on a blue mat that had seen better days. Her hips ached, sinking through the collapsed foam. Her ankles felt like dust ground into the floor. She heard the rising crash of a hundred comforted gasps as the rest returned to normal, giggling and chatting. Cathartic laughter of the kids around her. But she didn't laugh. Neither did the stranger, again a sixteen-year-old girl. She was alive; they both were. She saw her eyes again. LaShauna's brow was furrowed, and her eyes softened with concern. Adrian wiped the tears from her face and searched her shirt for blood. Nothing. She tried to breathe. Four seconds in… four seconds hold… four seconds out… four seconds hold…

"Are you alright?" Whatshername asked, unsure if she should stay, go, or call for help. Adrian held her hand to her collarbone, checking for blood. Her eyes glistened, and she dug her thumb and index finger in, gripping the bone through her skin before she let go with relief. She managed a half-smile, walking quickly back to the bleachers to sit in the back corner. Mr. Johnson gave some bullshit closing remarks after fighting to keep the rest of the group quiet. They giggled and whispered about their own moments of intimacy. As it approached, the thought of returning to their friends and loved ones and masks filled them with shuddering excitement. Their encounter was little more than a staring contest. When they were dismissed, a cacophony of cheers, laughter, and banter echoed against the walls as they crowded the doors and burst into the hallways to empty their lockers. The metallic banging echoed back through the halls as Adrian shuffled to the opposite door. She jogged to the bathroom outside the women's locker room and found a stall before she broke. She sobbed and wailed and coughed and wheezed until her chest was tired. Then she sat and sobbed silently until her face was sore, and her mom was texting her, wondering why she didn't come home on the bus.

# CYDNIE SUBMITS

A flashlight and a kitchen knife. That was all he could find that might be of any use. Cyd wondered if he was prepared, crazy, or on his way to his death. Maybe everyone had done this exact same thing. Maybe he was following the same script. Maybe they brought guns and Molotov cocktails and police backup. He was submitting, seeking out a thing that so desperately wanted to be found. Perhaps this was always its intent. He had pulled up a vent grate in Cambridge and started wandering the tunnels. There was no plan, no map, no chance. He would just wander and wander, hoping that if he had no plan, the terror wouldn't notice him. Maybe they all did, all the ones that came before him. Luckily, the T here was loud and slow, like the T everywhere. There would be no dramatic chases and last-minute dives into service access points. The last two cars of the evening have passed. Rumbling and scraping along with sparks coming from the top power cables, giving him plenty of time to hide from the sight of tired train operators, who undoubtedly would have stopped and sounded the alarm.

He'd wander for hours. No idea where to go, but it was somewhere here. There was no other way. He turned it over in his mind. For hours and hours, he had looked for an alternative. But Stacey was gone; no one else knew. No one would believe or care. He was alone. Something. A trap of some kind. What the hell was he looking for? The noise and voice that he'd known for so long was faint and in the distance. It hadn't found him yet. Cyd grinned broadly and tried to breathe. Ecstasy kept him hidden. It was the only way; somehow, the voice preyed on misery. Happiness, even artificial happiness, kept Cyd camouflaged. But how long it would last, or how well he'd stay hidden, was anyone's guess.

A day prior, he had finished reading Stacey's notebook and scoured her house for more information. She was gone. It was clear. Just a few weeks since she last wrote in the notebooks. The rest of the house had provided little help. All he found was the notebook; it reminded him of his own. Was this always part of the plan? Did they all write down their stories? It was in the sewers or the subway tunnels; that was clear. Her visions matched Cyd's. There were scraps of poetry and sketches of creeping horrors lurking in the shadows. Everything was so familiar. Cyd had to go. If he died, at least it was over.

He had already known that the uppers stopped the vision. A few months after Becca died, a friend offered him some ecstasy, and he felt chemical happiness for the first time. The voice, the god-awful voice that had nearly dragged him to hell, was suddenly quiet. He could feel the thing's attention wander, and he was hidden. E and Adderall kept him stable. He didn't know if the thing could actually read his mind or if it was just his own trauma. But it was searching for him. When he left Stacey's apartment, he resolved to end this, to find his ending. He loaded up on all the pills he had left. Taking them hourly. The tremors and euphoria kicked in right as he lifted that vent grate and slid his ragged corpse into the metro tunnels.

*Meat. Meat is here.*

Cyd felt the presence searching for him as he got closer. Visions of the hulking mass slithering along slimy tunnels of blood and slimes built up along slick concrete floors. Dripping from metal grates. He felt the cool air from above flow slowly through the tunnels as it mixed with the warm, soggy sewage airs of the depths. He felt the tunnels swell and contract like a living organism, and he felt the chaotic, interconnected presence of so many inhabitants.

It was searching. It felt him. It wanted him.

Arms twitching, desperately trying to vent the vibrant and destructive energy coursing through his capillaries, Cyd pressed on. He kept walking, even as his facial muscles seized and contorted his expression into what he only imagined may be a confusing and beguiled grimace. He tried to keep his body on task as he scuttled through the tunnels like Hunter S. Thompson.

He had trouble keeping the light steady, but it was the only way. He couldn't even find a decent flashlight. His phone had stopped working, and all he managed to find was one of those little keychains he had picked up at a bank. The pale blue glow seemed to make more shadows than it dispelled, but it was working. Everything was working. It still could not find him. He needed the drugs. They kept him hidden; they kept him safe.

Time eked by. Slower at every moment. He traveled through formless manmade caves for minutes, hours, and years. The sun gave up and would never rise again. The moon waned and sought to abandon him. The people he knew and loved were long gone, back in the corporeal realm. Awaiting their misery.

He slipped. Crossing through an intersection and finding a slick mud of filth lining the floor. He saw the world turn sideways and felt the heavy thud of his relaxed and unprepared body hit the ground. The world went dark, and he smiled up at the ceiling, enjoying the gentle caress of the filth on his scalp and back as it soaked through his clothes. "Why does my arm hurt?" He thought and tried to find his flashlight, which had hit the ground and rolled across the ground, pointing to the corner of a narrow passageway to his right, leaving him in darkness.

He envied his youth. As a kid, he had a lot less mass. Falls were common and minor. But he could feel his joints tweak and begin to swell. Then, the real pain set in. "Shit, I cut myself." His forearm felt odd, and he realized the flowing warmth along his elbow was blood puddling through the muck. He rolled onto his back and tried to sit up, but couldn't feel his hand move, only pain. He tried to grab it with his right hand to put pressure on the wound but felt a lightning strike through his arm and shoulder when he made contact with the handle of the kitchen knife, still lodged in between the bones of his forearm.

"Oh no." He thought weakly, still chuckling himself. The drugs coursed through his veins and out their escape route along the blade onto his jacket. He knew he shouldn't pull it out but didn't have a choice. He wiggled his fingers; the pain was there, but retreated to remain dull and distant. More importantly, his fingers moved. Just a little. Maybe he'd still have some function; the knife may have missed the tendons, just maybe. He dragged himself up to sit. Shuffling to the wall of the corridor with his good arm and kicking his feet. He couldn't take off his shirt to wrap the wound until he pulled the knife out. It would have to be quick. But if he moved too fast, he could sever a tendon or artery.

He grabbed the handle with his right hand and secured it tightly. Just a slow pull. The pressure built in his arm, and he felt a chill radiate through his spine and into his gut. He felt his stomach churn and was ready to vomit when the blade budged ever so slightly. He wretched and heaved his stomach out onto the floor. How far was that? He checked the blade in the light. He had only managed a half-inch; there was a lot more to go. He pulled again, but the progress was slow and slowing. This would never work. He couldn't pull it straight out. It pulled at an angle. If it came loose all of a sudden, he could sever something more important and bleed out before he reached the end.

He paused and tried to slow his breathing; The adrenaline was accelerating the dopamine rush into his system. He could feel the panicked racing of his heartbeat. But smiled at the tears streaming down his face, leaving lines of warm light across his cheeks. He looked up at the cold stone wall across from him. If he could use the wall to push the blade out, it would be straighter. He hoped the blade wouldn't bend. He closed his eyes and begged his heart to slow down, breathing with discipline. With his eyes still closed, briefly enjoying the floating sensation in his head and raising his wounded arm to shoulder level, he wedged the tip of the knife into a crack on the wall.

With his uninjured hand, he grabbed his left wrist and squared his shoulders. Using his body weight, he pressed his arm toward the wall. Crying out through his clenched teeth, holding back the urge to stop and vomit again. He pushed until he felt the weight shift in the knife and the horrible wrenching shock as the handle suddenly passed the tipping point and sagged toward the ground.

Release. His shoulders relaxed, and he rotated his wrist with the weight of the blade, giving way and letting it fall to the floor. The thin metal clatter on the concrete rang through the corridor and fell silent, belying the flurry of emotions that flooded his system. *Breathe, just breathe.* He rested his forehead on the wall and brought his awareness to his surroundings, which had all seemed to fade away in that instant. He tasted sour air, smelled the mildew and rot, heard distant drips of water echoing through the walls, and felt warm liquid dripping down his chin.

He raised his head and opened his eyes, realizing he had been resting his head on his injured arm, flowing freely over his face. The copper taste filled his mouth, and he rushed to slide off his jacket and t-shirt. The blood dripped down his elbow into his armpit and across his chest as he elevated it above his heart. He fumbled with the shirt, biting a hole in the sleeve and ripping it off of the torso. Roughly and rapidly, he wrapped and wrapped as tightly as he could. *Did the bleeding stop? Good enough.*

Gotta pick up the pace now. Who knows how much longer he had. He could still feel two fingers. It could be worse. He held the knife high above his head and continued through the dark path before him. *Not much time.*

∞ ∞ ∞

Around the corner, the pale moonlit glow of distant fluorescence echoed off the walls and revealed the messenger. The heap of moist flesh emanated a putrid wreak that clouded the tunnels and stung the eyes. Cyd felt the poison air waft through his lungs. He suppressed a gag that sent tingled through his gut and shoulders.

The beast, the rotten thing that unfolded before him, reveled in its own existence. It splayed out in the muck. Its light skin formed a rough silhouette like a crab's shell, hiding six atrophied legs that were nearly crushed under the weight of its opulence. It couldn't hold itself up, having glutted upon the nameless and faceless heaps of flesh delivered by the harvesting hordes. Its withered side legs dragged lifelessly as it scraped and slithered with its powerful front appendages. Too weak to lift its oversized body, it groped and dragged along the ground, leaving a horrible trail of slime, excrement, rotten flesh, and its own bile pasted along the floor. The whole tunnel system must be mapped by its trails, a terrible echo of its existence splayed out along the miles.

From the opposite side of the beast, Cyd heard the familiar clang and scuttle approach as the sharp-clawed terror of his dreams and waking nightmares clattered its way slowly out of the shadows. In its front mandibles, it carried a dripping mass covered in slime and dirt. From the formless silhouette, Cyd could discern a head and the better half of a torso with one arm severed at the bicep. The messenger paused and shivered in excitement when the rotten smell grew nearer. It extended its dragging body upward toward the delivery. Cyd finally perceived reality.

The messenger was no super beast or conniving genius. It chirped and whined at the approach of the other with the shuddering anticipation of a baby bird, and the traps of society were suddenly laid out before Cyd's eyes. The torment, the madness, and the terror he and who knows how many others faced was the impersonal entrapment of a predator. Neither good nor evil, just an animal. Somehow, this beast, this messenger, came to communicate. It learned to talk to people through their trauma and despair. All of his pain, all of his despair, was meaningless. *Ophelia died for nothing. Rebecca was a murderer.* Suddenly, the prey began to come to the nest. Were there others like it, or was it the one? He only ever heard the one voice, the grating, terrible voice in his head calling to him. But was it even a voice? Would a million more of these creatures all sound the same? It was even more likely that it sounded different to all of its victims. Each brain might perceive and resonate differently with whatever hellish frequency by which this thing communicated.

Cyd laughed and felt tears streaming down his face. *Ophelia died for nothing.* His utter hopelessness dawning on him and snuffing out the last light. There was no way to know if this would stop anything at all. *Ophelia died for nothing.* He was already dead. If he didn't overdose and have a heart attack, which seemed like a real possibility, as his heart pounded through his chest. Ophelia.

"Well, I'm here. *Ophelia died for nothing.* At least it will all be over for me." He thought, considering removing his bandage and letting himself bleed out. *Ophelia died for nothing.* The cutting *Ophelia* part is the painful *died* part. I'm pretty sure I'll just drift *nothing* away. Well, with my decreasing *Ophelia* blood pressure, *died* I'll probably have *for* a pretty significant *nothing* fear response. That *OPHELIA* sucks. Well, *DIED* between the E *FOR* and Adderall, adrenaline *NOTHING* is probably a better time to be had. At least I'll have given it a shot.

He tightened his grip on the sticky knife and waited.

The slurps and gurgles and crunches of the formless heap of human beings echoed. The reverberations off the walls ignited Cyd's ears and brain, reminding him of his folly and humanity. *OPHELIA DIED FOR NOTHING* To see someone who at once was the entire world reduced to a filthy object for the terror.

Its job done, the tall, clacking harvester turned its body in the cramped tunnel and scuttled into the darkness.

Cyd took a final breath. Push off from the wall, and stay quiet. Exhale slowly.

Don't drag the feet. Shift the weight to one side and lift off the ground.

Place the heel first; roll onto the toe.

The wet sloshing of the beast stifled the noise.

Again now, shift the weight. Heel, toe.

Heel, toe.

Heel, toe. *Ophelia died for nothing.*

Balance! He splayed his arms out to regain control. His left leg couldn't support his weight. He heard the faint scrape as he lowered his right leg to keep himself steady.

Silence.

The heaving beast was unaware.

He had to find a head. Or an artery? Something? It was all meat and shabby shells. Squishy and infinite in depth and volume.

Pausing until the squelching and cracking of bones resumes and echoed throughout the cavern. It muffled as the beast swallowed the last bits. Leaving its body to rest while it awaited its next meal.

Cyd moved forward; his opportunity was closing. Such tense excitement made him giddy. He felt a tickle trickle up to his face and escape his airway with a light chuckle.

Oh, the paradox of such fear and pleasure coinciding. Cyd saw God; he saw the universe for what it was in its chaotic, mathematical twisting and writhing against the walls.

Cyd saw God. Then, he met God. And God was a horrible, frail thing. Now, he had to kill God.

God was aware now; he knew him with the knife. It let out a horrible screech, like a terrified rabbit, that echoed off the walls. Weak, frail, and scared. But in his mind, Cyd heard the voice of God. The voice that had lured him all this was and tormented him for so long. But it didn't speak; it only screamed. The cacophony of a thousand braying animals and the low rumble of the world ending. *OPHELIA*

God had never known fear. *DIED* It never learned the words to plead for its life. *FOR NOTHING*

Action now. Cyd sprinted. He forgot about his injured leg, and it collapsed underneath him, slumping him back onto the sticky floor. Breathing through the pain, trying to clear his head. The *OP* cacophony broke *HEL* through the shield *IA* he had created for *DI* himself and *ED, and* the whole world *FOR* was on fire. His *NO* cellular walls seemed to decay *THING* and dissolve into mush. But he was there; he was alive. He had to kill God.

The creature wriggled and shook, dragging its filth away from him. Its plump, soft body slowly reaching out and scraping against the floor. He looked up and saw the thing slowly turned toward him. It wasn't running; it was trying to prey. He sh*O*ok his head and ke*P*t breat*H*ing. Lurching hims*EL*f onto h*I*s knees. Then his feet. This w*A*s it. In the *D*istance, he heard the fa*I*nt scr*E*eches an*D* echoes o*F* a d*O*zen mo*R*e horrors comi*N*g t*O* aid *TH*eir messenger. Cyd lunged aga*I*n and plu*N*Ged his knife in between its bulbous eyes.

God didn't want to die; God wanted to eat. It groped and slashed wildly with its mandibles and chomped with its razor teeth.

Cyd stabbed and stabbed. Looking for a weak spot he couldn't find. Desperately trying to keep the rest of his body away from the razor teeth.

He stabbed and stabbed. He chopped at the protruding eyes and severed the putrid thing from the hulking body. Thick black liquid poured from God and covered him. He could no longer distinguish between his body and God's. Still, he heaved and pushed and stabbed.

The cacOphony of the monster Penetrated His psychE and reached his nerves. Cyd was aLive, but hIs light fAded. He was dying. The messenger had become a part of him. With every heave, Cyd felt the knife in his skull. He was killing himself. *So what if it's true. Ophelia died for nothing. He doesn't even know what a baby is.* He stabbed and stabbed; only one would survive. There was no rift between his existence and his foe's. He couldn't see his body. Was he subsumed, or was he blindly stabbing himself in the face? No way to tell. If Cyd was God, God had to die. So, he stabbed again.

Thick black liquid filled the room and threatened to drown them both. Cyd had seen the abyss and knew it was where they belonged. And so, he stabbed. He lunged and slashed and wailed.

He felt something in his own body. It was his and not the things. It was his own. And suddenly, he knew he was Cyd and not God. Horrible pain in his chest. Pressure on his right leg.

"A heart attack," he thought. He looked at his leg; it wasn't God's, just Cyd's, with a horrible claw-like mandible wrapped around his ankle.

As he looked, he saw his body separate from the beast's. They were apart, and the sound was fading. He recognized his existence, but the beast was not done. It squeezed and, with a crack, severed Cyd's foot at the ankle.

But Cyd felt no pain. He had become God. God was dead, and he was God. His crimson blood glowed hot and showered them, mixing with God's. And. He.. Felt... Release..... The........ Thing..... Was... Dead. His. Mind.. Was... Quiet..... And........ The..... World... Calmed.

Cyd shoved and separated his body from the beast. Intestines slithered from his gut, quiet and wet as they splattered on the dusty floor. He felt nothing as viscera poured from his torso, and he fell backward and saw no light in the ceiling as he waited for his journey to end with a sudden stop at the bottom.

But there was no pain; there was peace. And as Cyd's mind drifted into nothingness, he heard the faint screams of the harvesting terrors as they beheld the corpse of their God.

# THE ESCAPE

James kept his eyes closed as long as he could. 'No god damn it,' not again. The sleep had turned to naps. The naps turned to shorter and shorter collapses in desperation. At first, there was rest, but as it shrank, even the fragile balance of uneasy sleep was invaded by flashing horrors. Dreams of loneliness, despair. Flashes of sharp blades and disemboweled corpses. A scream, a shock, the sharp pop of a skull exploding on a funeral pyre. Images and sounds that thrust him awake but were always just out of reach when he tried to remember them. It wasn't enough that he only slept a few minutes at a time. His mind seemed to revolt in his escape, determined to make his waking nightmares preferable to his dreams.

James hadn't heard from Cyd in weeks, and he was worried. Not worried enough to call the police, but creeping thoughts invaded his peace during the brief, and much needed, respites from diaper changes, bottle warming, and foot massaging. It kept him awake, shortening his micro-naps on the couch. 'Fucking Cyd doesn't even have the decency to check in with me, so I know he's fucking alive.' But Cyd felt like a burden, and not without reason. He probably wouldn't reach out ever again if James didn't do it first. Honestly, it would be a lie to say James wasn't a little relieved that he didn't have to make emotional room for him anyway. After all, he had been thinking about how their relationship would change after the baby was born. Cyd tried so hard not to resent him. But in the end, James resented him just as much. He tried to be a good friend but had to pretend that he wasn't happy or excited for the baby when Cyd was around, and he hated associating the joy of his child with the guilt of Cyd's.

But it wasn't Cyd's fault. No matter how tough he got to be around. It was Becca. Becca destroyed him, body and soul. James was the only person that still showed up for coffee instead of avoiding him altogether, lest Cyd suck them all into his misery. James just wished he had someone like Cyd had had in him. Someone who at least cared, someone who could handle it if he unloaded a few problems now and again. Is that fatherhood? To support, not be supported, and after just a few weeks, James understood Cyd better than ever. When Ophelia was born, Cyd sent pictures and doted and beamed as people paraded into his house to see her. But visits waned. They needed space. Becca needed rest. James didn't want to be impolite, even when Cyd had withdrawn completely. Cyd had disappeared. He ended conversations quickly, like the fading smile of a half-hearted joke. James wanted to give him space; let him focus on his family. He knew it was something he couldn't understand.

When he did see Cyd again, it was in passing as he scraped his feet along the sidewalks on the way to the drugstore for some necessity, floating like a wraith, drifting through crowds but never making an impact on the pedestrians around him. He was withered, translucent. James tried to connect, but Cyd was cut off. Never looking him quite in the eye. James remembered fondly the old cures… there was nothing a rooftop view and a cheap bottle of vodka couldn't drown. They would play music on a cracked speaker and drink until they couldn't feel the world anymore. They couldn't feel the disappointment. They would prowl the streets, wandering into parties, checking for unlocked cars, and harassing anyone who would pay attention. They would fight and run and laugh and cry and scream until they passed out. In the morning, they woke up, sometimes together, sometimes separately, soaked in piss, vomit, and condensation on the scratchy shingled roof of an apartment several blocks away. Enough physical pain had a way of drowning out the invisible. When it got worse, they would rinse and repeat.

When Cyd had Ophie, there was no medicine that could make the world seem alright again. He mumbled to James on a hot summer night, after half of the bottle of bourbon as they looked across the city to the interstate in the distance, the bits of shingles breaking off of the porch roof beneath them and collecting in the creases of their belts and under shirts. "How fucking unlucky is she?"

"What do you mean?"

"Can you imagine having no other choice but to count on this guy to raise you? Short straw."

"You'll do fine. Humans have survived this long with much worse fathers than you."

"Maybe." Cyd never brought it up again. But he left early that morning and James didn't hear from him for two weeks. Sarah assured him, held his hand, and told him Cyd was just taking his job more seriously, trying to be a good dad. We just needed to give him some space.

That's what everyone was doing for James now, wasn't it? But family life, the terrifying microcosm of the universe, kept him awake much more than the desperate screams of baby David. The universe was different, and he was trapped. A desperate guardian trying to protect his baby from the savage and hungry world, knowing full well there was no hope and no help coming. His family, his friends, and even Cyd was leaving him alone. Their misguided altruism cut him off from a rational perspective and left him a prisoner to sudden conceptual flights that stirred fear and panic in his heart. He couldn't share the worry or anger or shame with Sarah; she was tired. Too tired to entertain any long conversations about it. And for the past few weeks, too tired to communicate more than a grunt about anything.

Instead, he sat quietly and smiled on cue. He had learned to smile with his eyes, and no one seemed to know the difference. He repeated his last conversation with Cyd over and over in his head. He remembered in shame how tired he felt, how resentful. How much he wanted to tell Cyd to grow up and move on. Now, the words echoed in his head.

*Do you ever feel chained by your own existence? The very body and mind that define you are the architects of your limitation. It's like everything else in the infinite spectrum. In order to exist, we must be carved, separated, and defined relative to the rest. In order for something to be, it must also not be. That is, it must be different from something else. So, existence is inherently relativistic. It is a relationship between two things. If there is only one, there is nothing. The structure of the mind and body only exist because they are limited. They only have meaning because they cannot achieve all things.*

James slumped onto his couch and stared at the muted weather report. Nothing has meaning on its own. So, he would fight and die in the service of the ones he loved. Even if they were just as meaningless as he was. He valued them above all others. He reinforced this every night before drifting off to a sweaty and semi-conscious sleep. He repeated it to himself every morning while rolling to loosen his aching spine. Sarah needed him, David needed him, and there was nothing that would prevent that.

His old wife died in childbirth, and her body transformed into the hulking and slithering mass of hair and tears that haunted the house from the bedroom to the bathroom. Sarah was a solemn, pitiful, dangerous thing. He desperately tried to relieve her burden. He tried to take the baby away as much as possible so she could sleep, or shower, or go to the store. When he let his guard down, he heard real or imagined sobs coming from the bedroom door and rushed to the bedroom in a panic. Only to find her weeping quietly and covering her head, staring at the bassinet.

Her labor was quick and traumatic. No epidural, no time, twenty minutes of labor, an emergency c-section, hours of terror and anxiety, and there was a human. A tiny human that sat on a warming table next to her unconscious body for hours. James sat, useless and helpless, not knowing who to comfort, who to touch, and who to worry about. He stood over them as the sun rose and fell, as his neck seized and his back creaked. The tiny hands of his new son gripped his index finger while he rested his hand on his wife's face, waiting for the moment when her breathing stopped. He checked her breath every moment, staring at her chest, praying it would rise and fall again *just one more time*.

The bleeding wasn't stopping. Hours went by, and they couldn't stop the bleeding. They checked on her every fifteen minutes, and the bleeding just wouldn't stop. The doctors warned him not to go into the adjacent bathroom lest he see the blood pads and wind up emotionally scarred or traumatized somehow. He wallowed in mingled bliss and terror, wondering if he had the fortitude to raise Davey alone. Every time he walked down the hall to the visitors' bathroom, he passed screaming children, happy couples getting discharged, and visions of returning to his wife's still body. She stirred on day two. She made eye contact on day three. A faint smile was like a shot of adrenaline in his chest, and he prepared them to return home. She looked at David, and her eyes glossed. To work so hard, for so long, for such a little thing, warm in his plastic chamber. The tiny monster that tried to kill his wife. He could never forget that thought.

David was so quiet. Even his cries seemed muted and polite. He slept on that heated table, bathed in multicolored lights. Waiting for his chance to exist. Or perhaps he missed the womb after being thrust so dramatically into the cruel world. His skin was wrinkled and thin. Weak, soft, bony little fingers clasped around James' nose when he held him up to his face. James sniffed his skin, hoping to find love. It wasn't as happy as he had hoped. His love was lined with fear. The crushing pressure of responsibility.

Weeks went by, and Sarah was quiet. Their bedroom had all the grandeur and coziness of a broom closet. The already low ceilings seemed to cave in when they installed black-out curtains. The piercing ray of light along the sides cut the small four-post bed in half and illuminated the cold, white bathroom. The cracked tiles and chipped mirror of a well-worn city apartment. She often sat on the edge of the bed. Holding baby David, staring out the window and crying. James wondered how he could tell if she was losing it. But he stifled his panic and gave her the biggest, warmest hug he could fake. He called her beautiful and took the boy. He couldn't tell her that he combed his memory for any warning signs Rebecca may have shown. He went through every story Cyd ever told and memorized every possible indicator of suicidal or homicidal thoughts. Sarah would be ruined; she would never trust him again. She would never trust herself again. But the more he lied, the more important the lie became. The more important the lie became, the more transparent it was.

James had quietly disposed of the razors. He upgraded them to electric only and eyed the chipped corners of the mirror and the cracked tiles every time he brushed his teeth. Was it that shape before? Was there anything missing? Was she ready to strike? Was today the day? Was today the day he came home to a pair of corpses? He hoped that, at the very least, he came home to just one corpse.

So, James hid it all underneath; maybe someday, when they were through this, he'd see a counselor. But not today, not alone. So, he quietly occupied himself with worries and distractions. Where was Cyd? Was he gone forever this time? The news droned on in the background as he poured a bowl of cereal and warmed up a packet of breast milk for David. He never remembered what they said on the TV. His mind was elsewhere. Something about violent murders and abductions on the rise. Pretty typical these days. Crazy people spouting conspiracies about monsters roaming the streets at night. James knew his brain had stopped working weeks ago. He only slept about an hour a night. Sooner or later, you start to hallucinate.

What would happen when his parental leave ended? Would she be better by then? He eyed the cracked bedroom door. He turned down the thermostat and wrapped the couch blanket over his shoulders. Sarah slept better when it was cold. She wrapped herself in all of the blankets and hibernated in her cocoon. Then he turned to survey the small apartment he had been so proud of two years ago. It now was stuffed and crowded; the air was thick and moist. He opened the window out to the brisk December. The dusting of snow from the night before had already melted and browned on the streets, creating muddy little rivers and flushing the filth into the storm drains. He glanced over his shoulder at Davey sleeping in the pack-and-play, unmoving. He pulled the pack of cigarettes hidden behind the bookshelf and crawled out the window onto the fire escape.

The brisk air engulfed him and wrapped itself around his bare chest. The cold, sharp steel of the metal grate stabbed his shoeless feet and sent the deep pain of cold into his bones. He fished out the lighter from the pack and lit up, feeling the reassuring wave of nicotine penetrate his lungs and enter his bloodstream. The pain of the world was infinite and enthralling, reminding him of the limits of his animal body. He looked down at the pedestrians beginning to emerge on the streets below. He saw their paths and destinations and thoughts and dreams swirl around them as they trudged across the treacherous ice slush that Boston had provided. A few noticed him and stared, wondering if he was a crazy person about to jump. "No, just crazy," he imagined them saying as they moved on and avoided further eye contact.

He escaped the cold and crouched back through the window into the living room. He rinsed out his mouth in the bathroom before returning to his coffee and cereal. A soft shuffling noise and grunting warned him of Davey's imminent crying fit. So, James rushed to the crib before the noise woke up Sarah. He fed and cleaned the boy, feeling the weight of his son in his hands and silently saying his daily pledge to keep him safe. Then he laid him on his chest while he stared at the ceiling, listening to more news reports. He danced with the idea of more sleep, entering a semi-hallucinogenic state of half-consciousness. The reporters spoke of great hulking beasts emerging from the sewers and subway stations, homeless people, and drunks and junkies reporting strange disappearances. The nightmares wouldn't stop, and the world would end. All his dreams ended that way recently.

Sarah got to sleep in today. She desperately needed it. So did he, but it was worth it when she finally emerged at noon. The blackout curtains gave the room a distorted sense of time, like entering a wormhole, even before he caught her stapling them to the walls last week to snuff out the last rays of sunlight. When she finally shuffled out in her underwear and a t-shirt, she stretched her arms upward, revealing her cesarian wound, almost healed. As she yawned and groaned in pain, she opened her eyes slightly and saw him on the couch, cradling the baby and watching her softly. She smiled for the first time in weeks, and tears welled in James' eyes. Hope kindled itself like the last desperate fire in a darkening cave. He smiled back, careful not to disturb the baby.

"Good morning," he mouthed.

She finished her stretch and shuffled into the bathroom. "Good morning, babe," she replied softly. The light clicked on, and the old city pipes groaned for a moment before the steady rush of water erupted and broke the silence. Steam cautiously trickled out of the open doorframe. James heard her fumble with the mirror and start brushing her teeth. His heart began to slow, and he relaxed for the first time in months as she took care of herself without him having to drag her and argue. He looked away, back at the TV where they interviewed the city's public health commissioner. She was commenting on some chart that displayed a large graph. The screen read *correlation between a rise in abductions and a fall in suicides.*

'Not today. Today is a good day,' James thought as he switched the channel to football and looked down at his baby boy, fast asleep suckling, dreaming of another bottle. He felt warmth again and settled into the couch as a father.

"Goodbye, Cyd." He thought as his smile dissolved, sinking into a frown that threatened to swallow him up. He shifted in his seat and laid on his back, closing his eyes and feeling the soft weight of his son shift on his chest.

## ABOUT THE AUTHOR

Dan Dillenback is a poet at heart who spends most of his time writing prose for work. He considers himself an aging punk (he stopped moshing when he became the oldest one in the pit). He describes himself as a paradox, a career Army officer with a problem with authority, or sometimes just a nerd. He never quite figured out what he wants to do when he grows up, leading to an eclectic education. He has a bachelor's in advertising, and three master's degrees in Geological Engineering, Military Arts and Sciences, and Public Administration. He is an advocate for mental health in the military and has used writing and music to manage his anxiety and ADHD for most of his life.

Dan grew up in Western Massachusetts but has traveled the country since 2011 with his wife and children. They most recently settled in Northern Virginia.